# 降去神通

# AVATAR

## THE LAST AIRBENDER.

## Aang's Unfreezing Day

CREATED BY
**BRYAN KONIETZKO**
**MICHAEL DANTE DIMARTINO**

降击神通

# AVATAR
## THE LAST AIRBENDER
### Aang's Unfreezing Day

SCRIPT
**KELLY LEIGH MILLER**

ART AND COVER
**DIANA SIM** with
**CHRISTIANNE GILLENARDO-GOUDREAU**

COLORS
**MICHAEL ATIYEH**

LETTERING
**RICHARD STARKINGS &**
**Comicraft's JIMMY BETANCOURT**

COVER ART
**DIANA SIM**

DARK HORSE BOOKS

PRESIDENT AND PUBLISHER **MIKE RICHARDSON**

EDITOR **RACHEL ROBERTS**     ASSOCIATE EDITOR **JENNY BLENK**

ASSISTANT EDITOR **ANASTACIA FERRY**     DESIGNER **SARAH TERRY**

DIGITAL ART TECHNICIAN **SAMANTHA HUMMER**

Special thanks to James Salerno and Jeff Whitman at Nickelodeon, to
Michael Dante DiMartino, Bryan Konietzko, and Joan Hilty at Avatar Studios, and to Tim Hedrick.

**Nickelodeon Avatar: The Last Airbender™—Aang's Unfreezing Day**

Published by
Dark Horse Books
A division of Dark Horse Comics LLC
10956 SE Main Street | Milwaukie, OR 97222

DarkHorse.com | Nick.com

To find a comics shop in your area, visit comicshoplocator.com

First edition: January 2023
ISBN 978-1-50672-661-8 | eBOOK ISBN 978-1-50672-664-9

1 3 5 7 9 10 8 6 4 2
Printed in China

Neil Hankerson Executive Vice President • Tom Weddle Chief Financial Officer • Dale LaFountain Chief Information Officer • Tim Wiesch Vice President of Licensing • Matt Parkinson Vice President of Marketing • Vanessa Todd-Holmes Vice President of Production and Scheduling • Mark Bernardi Vice President of Book Trade and Digital Sales • Randy Lahrman Vice President of Product Development • Ken Lizzi General Counsel • Dave Marshall Editor in Chief • Davey Estrada Editorial Director • Chris Warner Senior Books Editor • Cary Grazzini Director of Specialty Projects • Lia Ribacchi Art Director • Matt Dryer Director of Digital Art and Prepress • Michael Gombos Senior Director of Licensed Publications • Kari Yadro Director of Custom Programs • Kari Torson Director of International Licensing

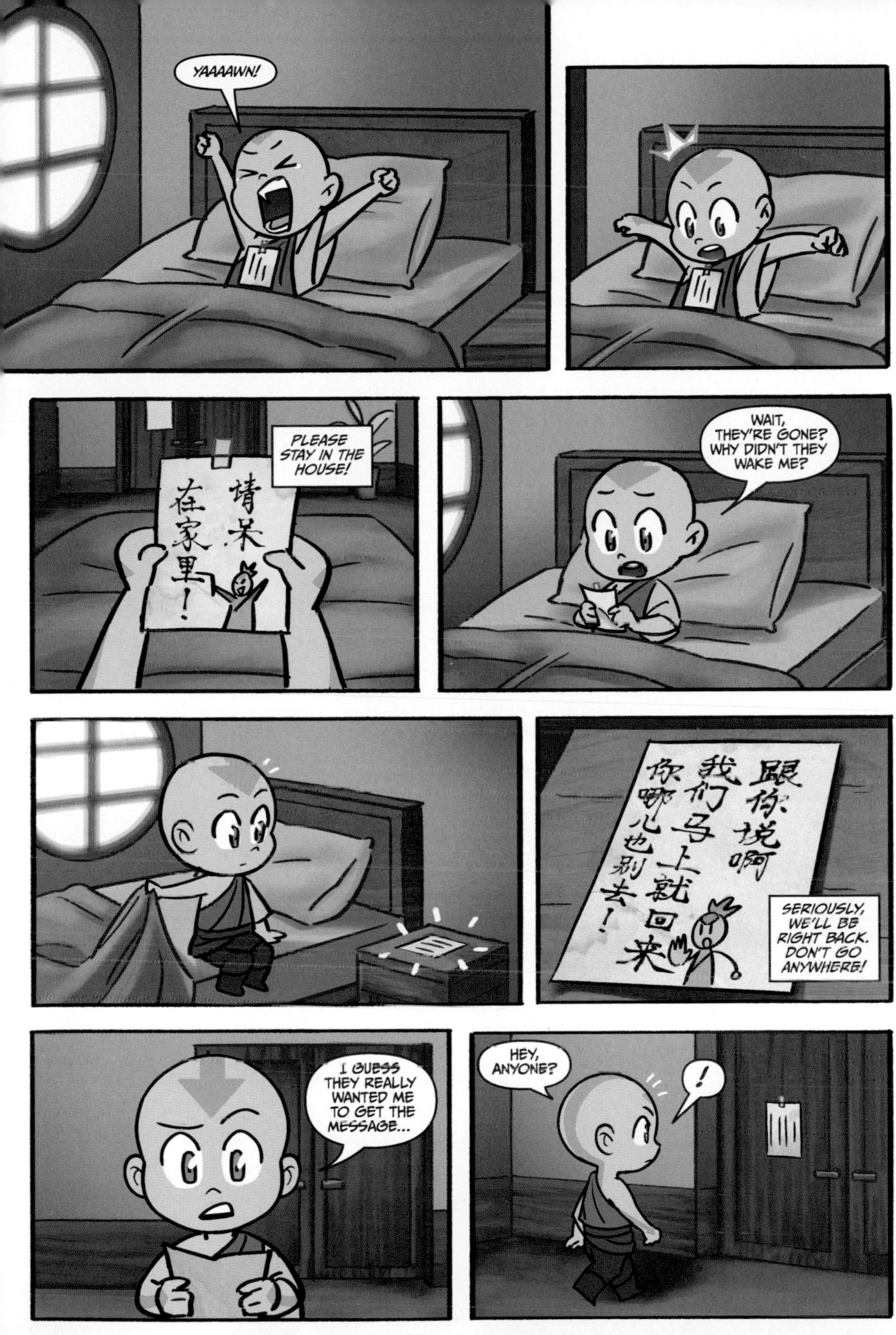
YAAAAWN!
请呆
在家里！
PLEASE STAY IN THE HOUSE!
WAIT, THEY'RE GONE? WHY DIDN'T THEY WAKE ME?
跟你说啊
我们马上就回来
你哪儿也别去！
SERIOUSLY, WE'LL BE RIGHT BACK. DON'T GO ANYWHERE!
I GUESS THEY REALLY WANTED ME TO GET THE MESSAGE...
HEY, ANYONE?
!

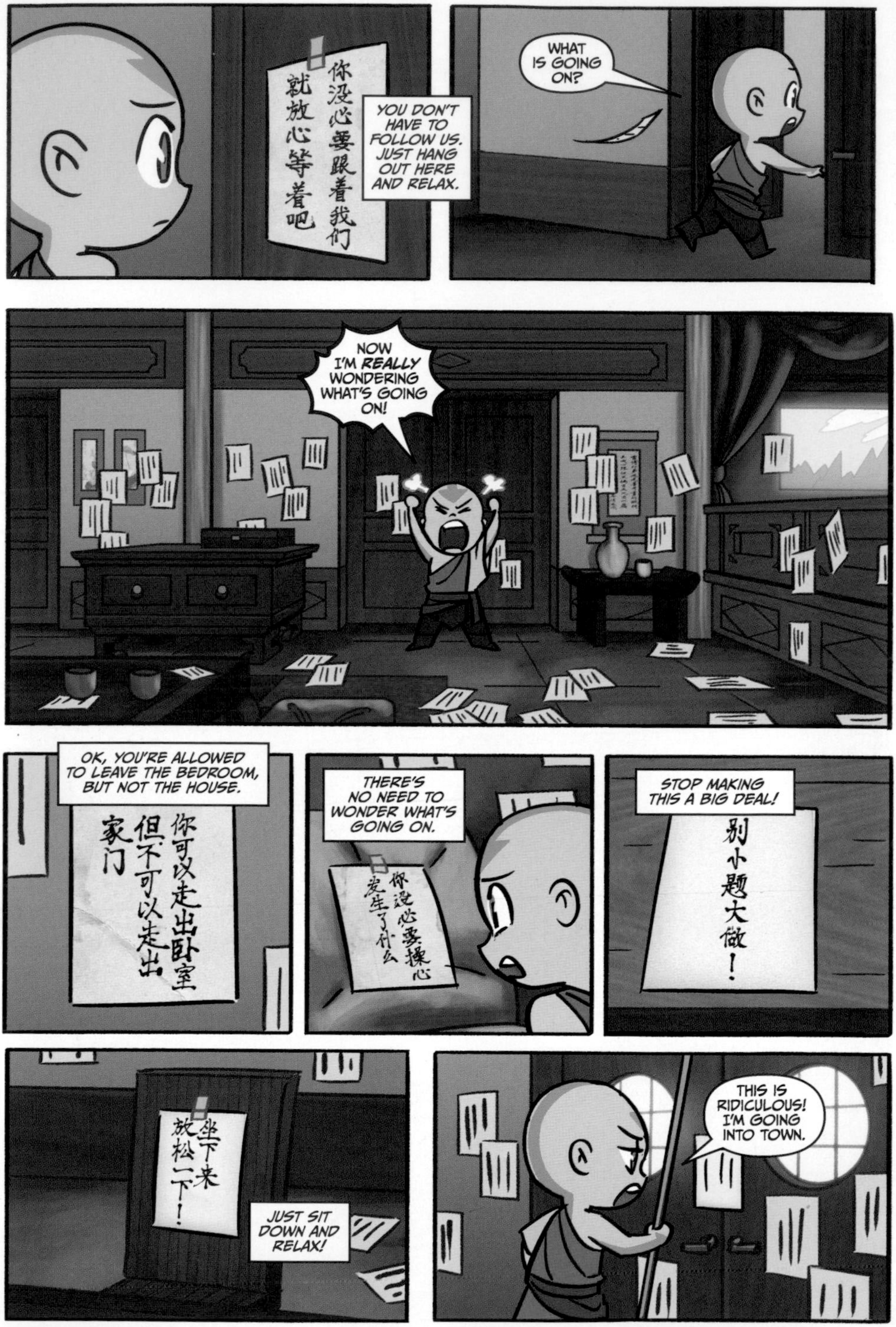
你没心要跟着我们
就放心等着吧
YOU DON'T HAVE TO FOLLOW US. JUST HANG OUT HERE AND RELAX.
WHAT IS GOING ON?
NOW I'M *REALLY* WONDERING WHAT'S GOING ON!
OK, YOU'RE ALLOWED TO LEAVE THE BEDROOM, BUT NOT THE HOUSE.
你可以走出卧室
但不可以走出
家门
THERE'S NO NEED TO WONDER WHAT'S GOING ON.
你没心要操心
发生了什么
STOP MAKING THIS A BIG DEAL!
别小题大做！
坐下来
放松一下！
JUST SIT DOWN AND RELAX!
THIS IS RIDICULOUS! I'M GOING INTO TOWN.

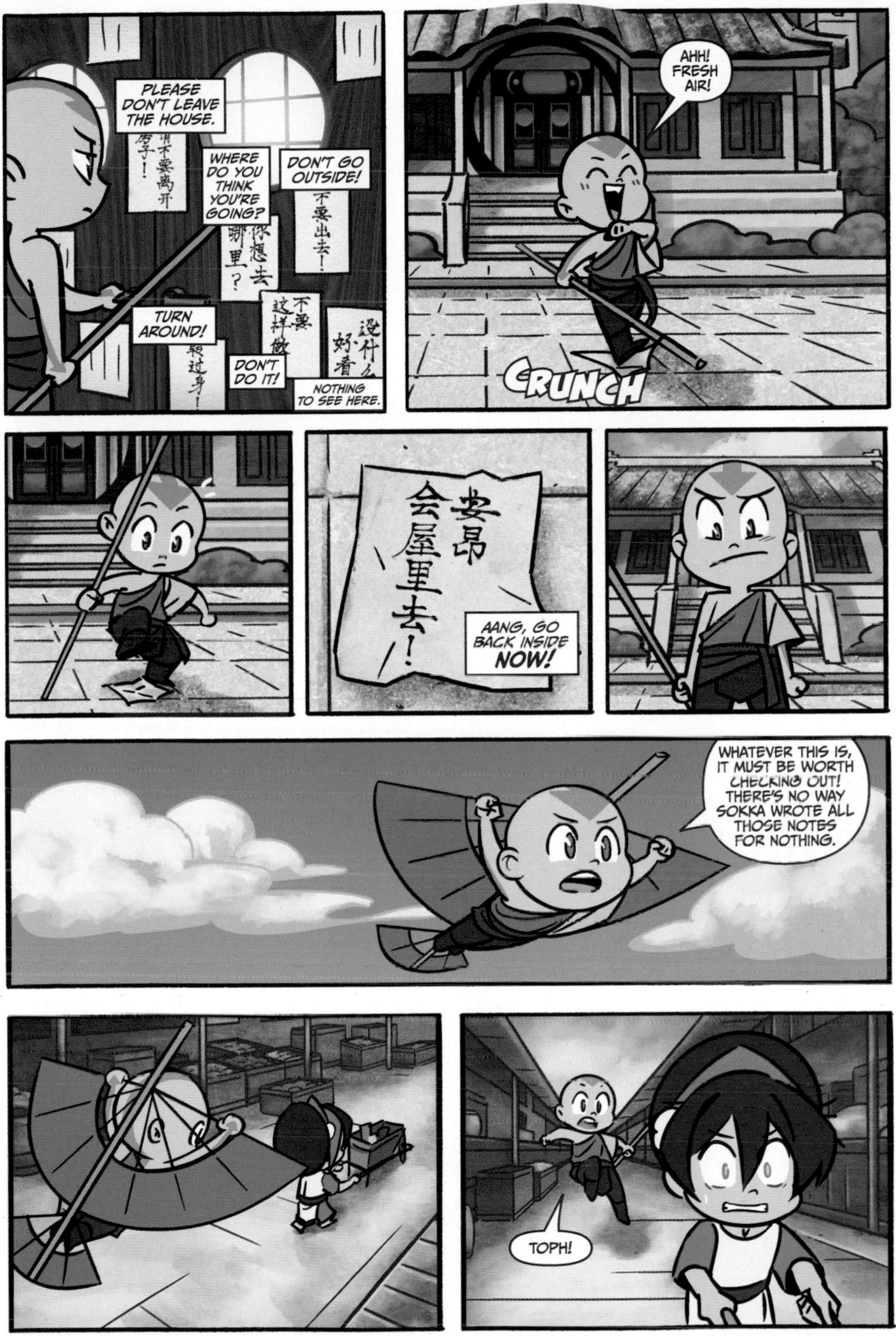

PLEASE DON'T LEAVE THE HOUSE.
WHERE DO YOU THINK YOU'RE GOING?
你想去哪里？
DON'T GO OUTSIDE!
不要出去！
TURN AROUND!
DON'T DO IT!
不要这样做
NOTHING TO SEE HERE.
AHH! FRESH AIR!
CRUNCH
安昂会屋里去！
AANG, GO BACK INSIDE NOW!
WHATEVER THIS IS, IT MUST BE WORTH CHECKING OUT! THERE'S NO WAY SOKKA WROTE ALL THOSE NOTES FOR NOTHING.
TOPH!

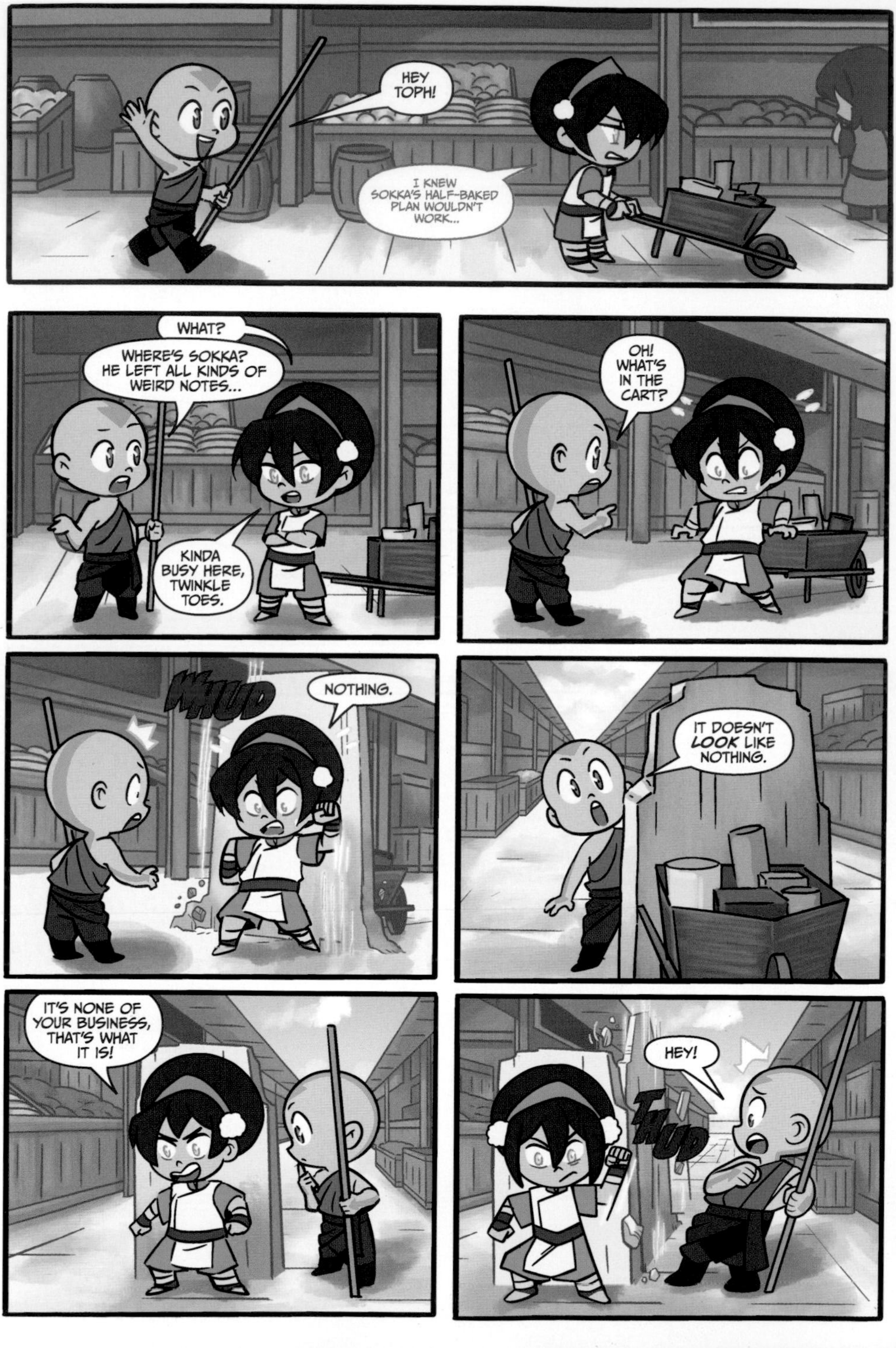
HEY TOPH!
I KNEW SOKKA'S HALF-BAKED PLAN WOULDN'T WORK...
WHAT?
WHERE'S SOKKA? HE LEFT ALL KINDS OF WEIRD NOTES...
KINDA BUSY HERE, TWINKLE TOES.
OH! WHAT'S IN THE CART?
WHUD
NOTHING.
IT DOESN'T LOOK LIKE NOTHING.
IT'S NONE OF YOUR BUSINESS, THAT'S WHAT IT IS!
HEY!
THUD

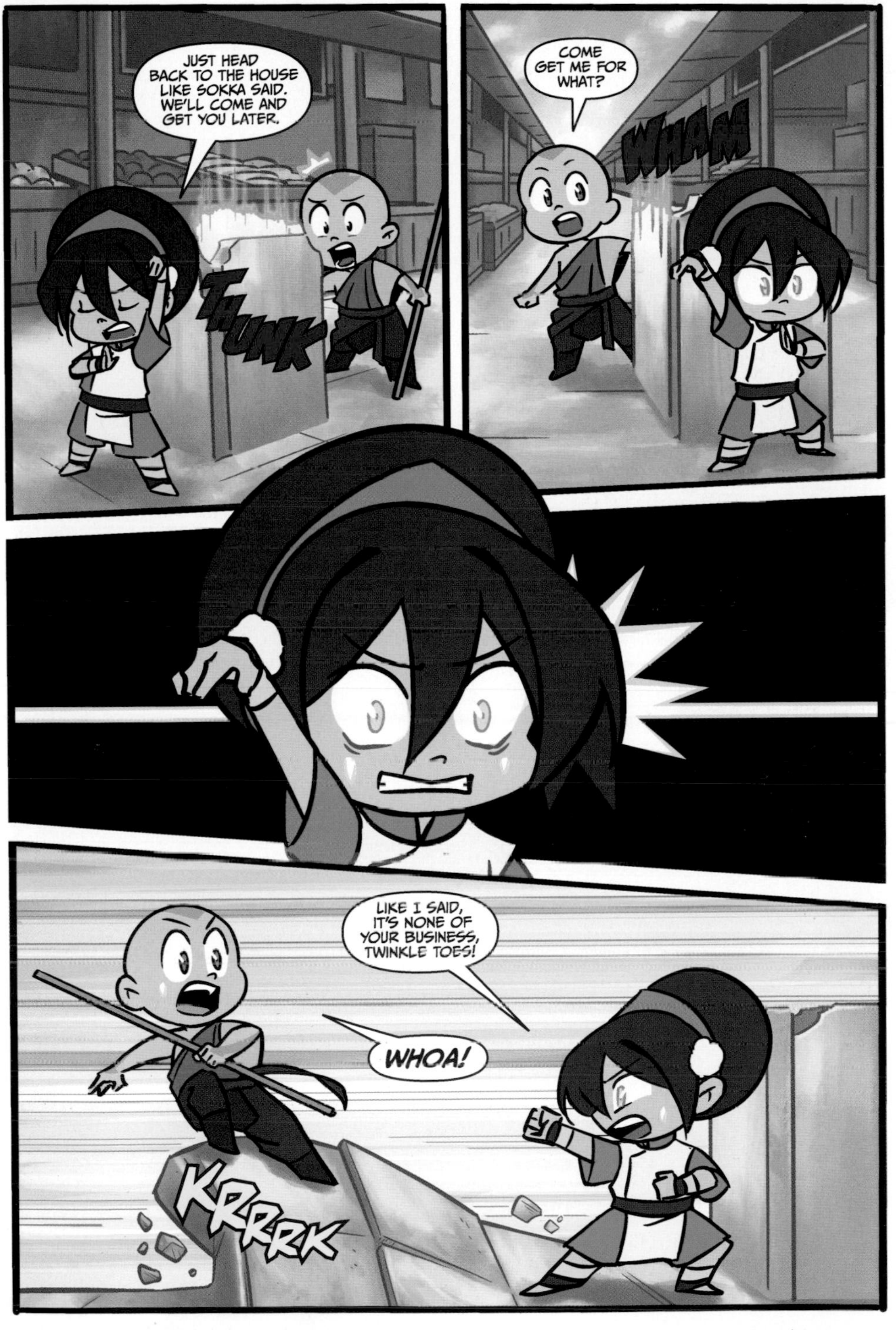
JUST HEAD BACK TO THE HOUSE LIKE SOKKA SAID. WE'LL COME AND GET YOU LATER.
THUNK
COME GET ME FOR WHAT?
WHAM
LIKE I SAID, IT'S NONE OF YOUR BUSINESS, TWINKLE TOES!
WHOA!
KRRRK

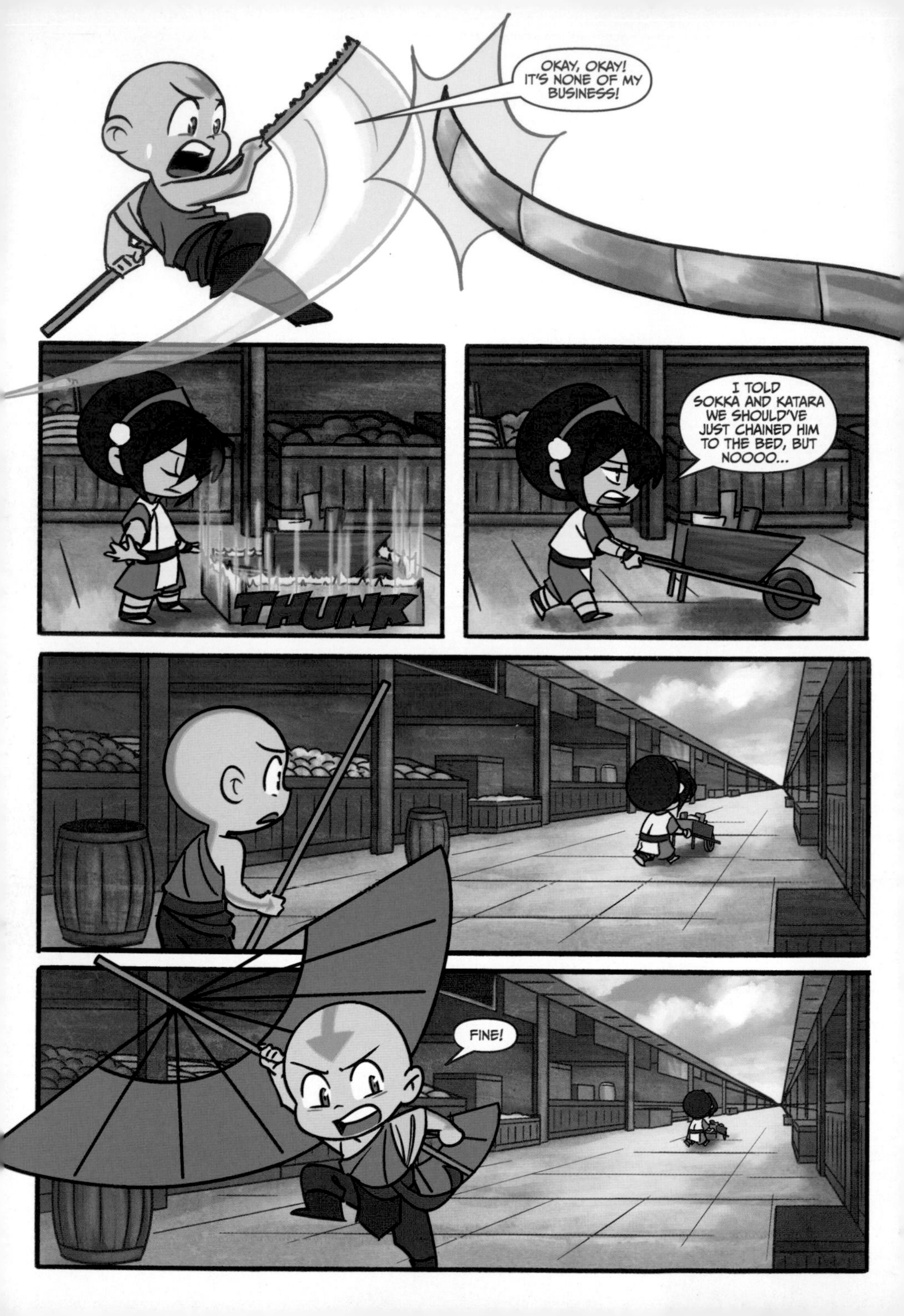
OKAY, OKAY! IT'S NONE OF MY BUSINESS!
THUNK
I TOLD SOKKA AND KATARA WE SHOULD'VE JUST CHAINED HIM TO THE BED, BUT NOOOO...
FINE!

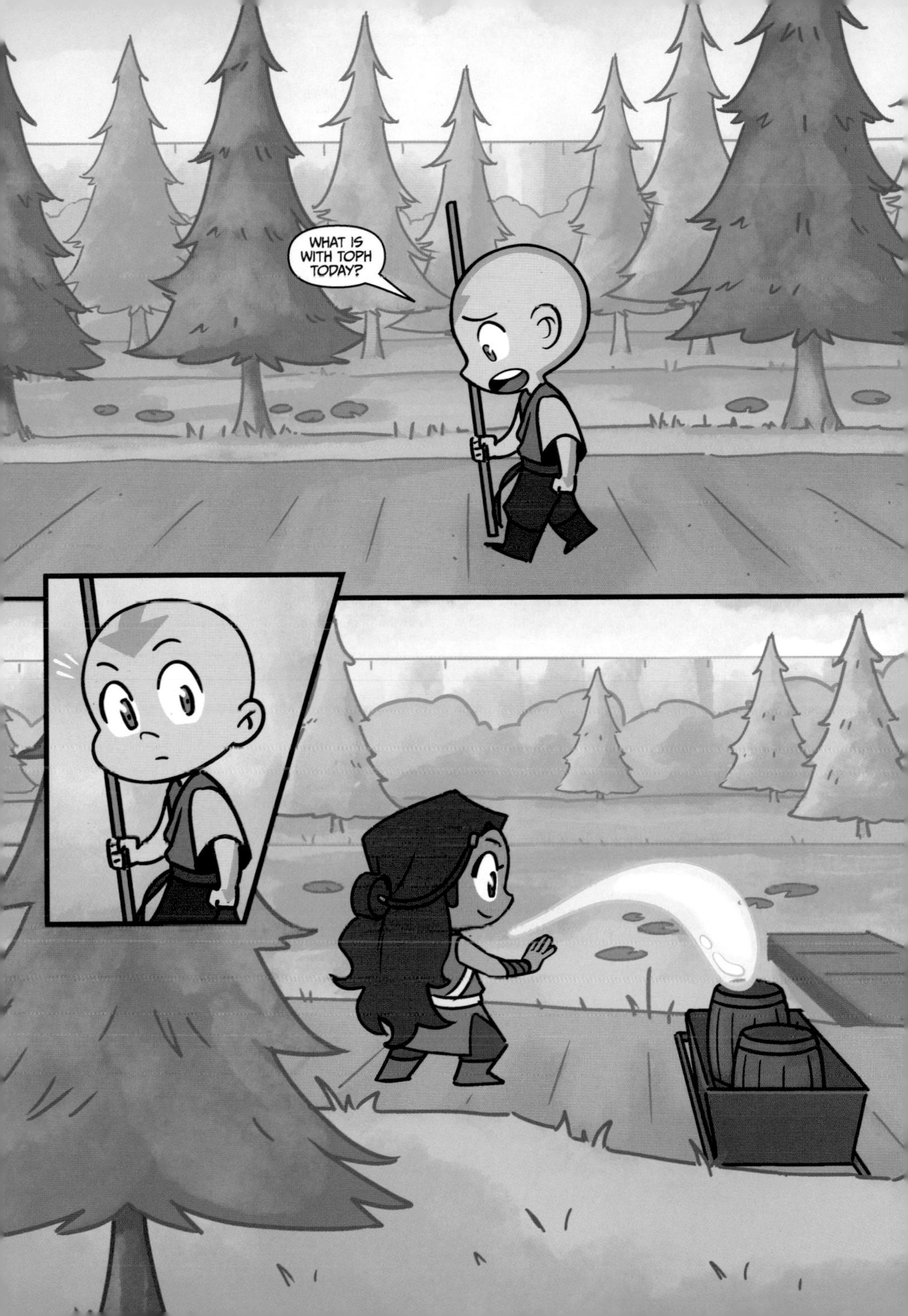
WHAT IS WITH TOPH TODAY?

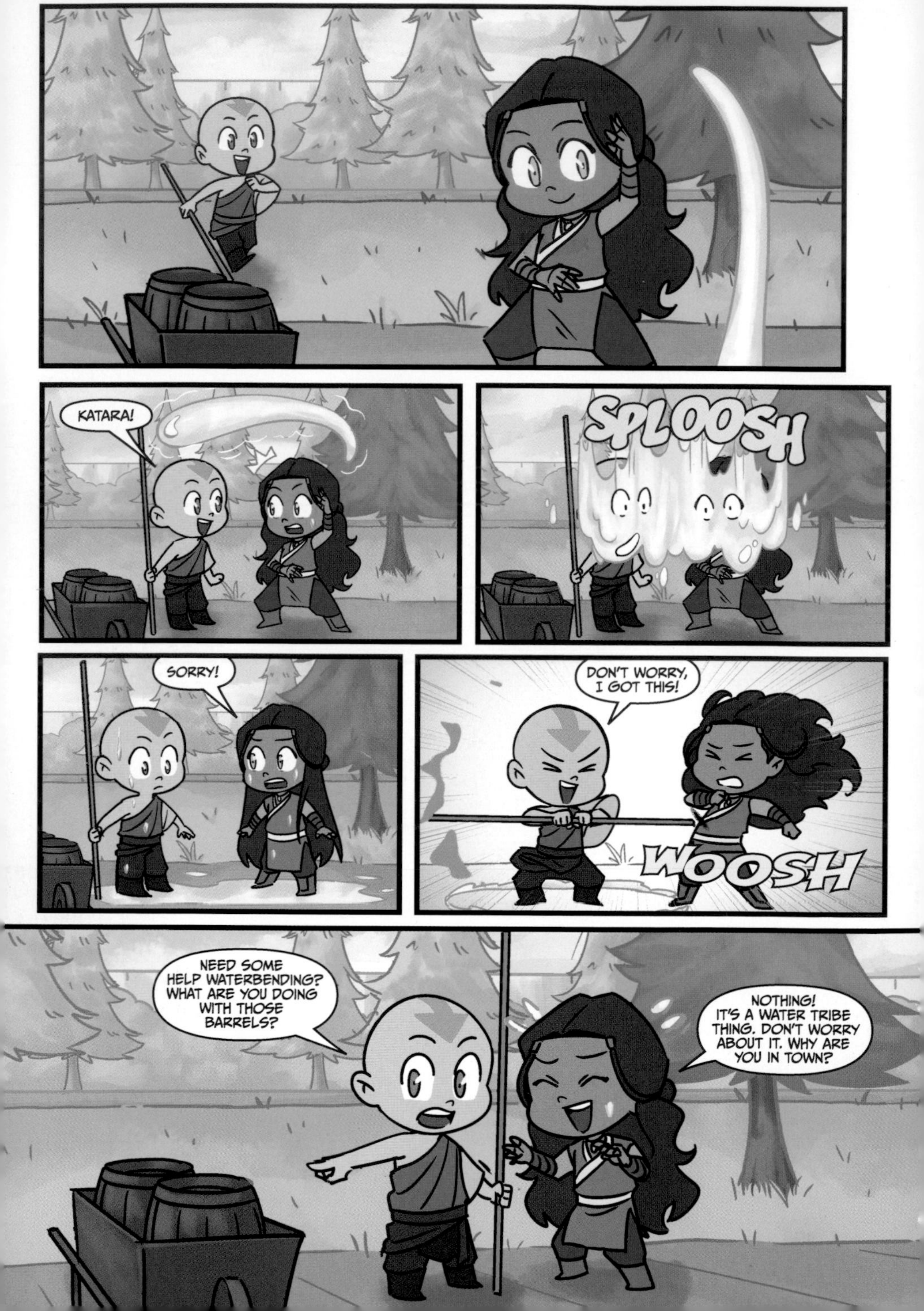
KATARA!
SPLOOSH
SORRY!
DON'T WORRY, I GOT THIS!
WOOSH
NEED SOME HELP WATERBENDING? WHAT ARE YOU DOING WITH THOSE BARRELS?
NOTHING! IT'S A WATER TRIBE THING. DON'T WORRY ABOUT IT. WHY ARE YOU IN TOWN?

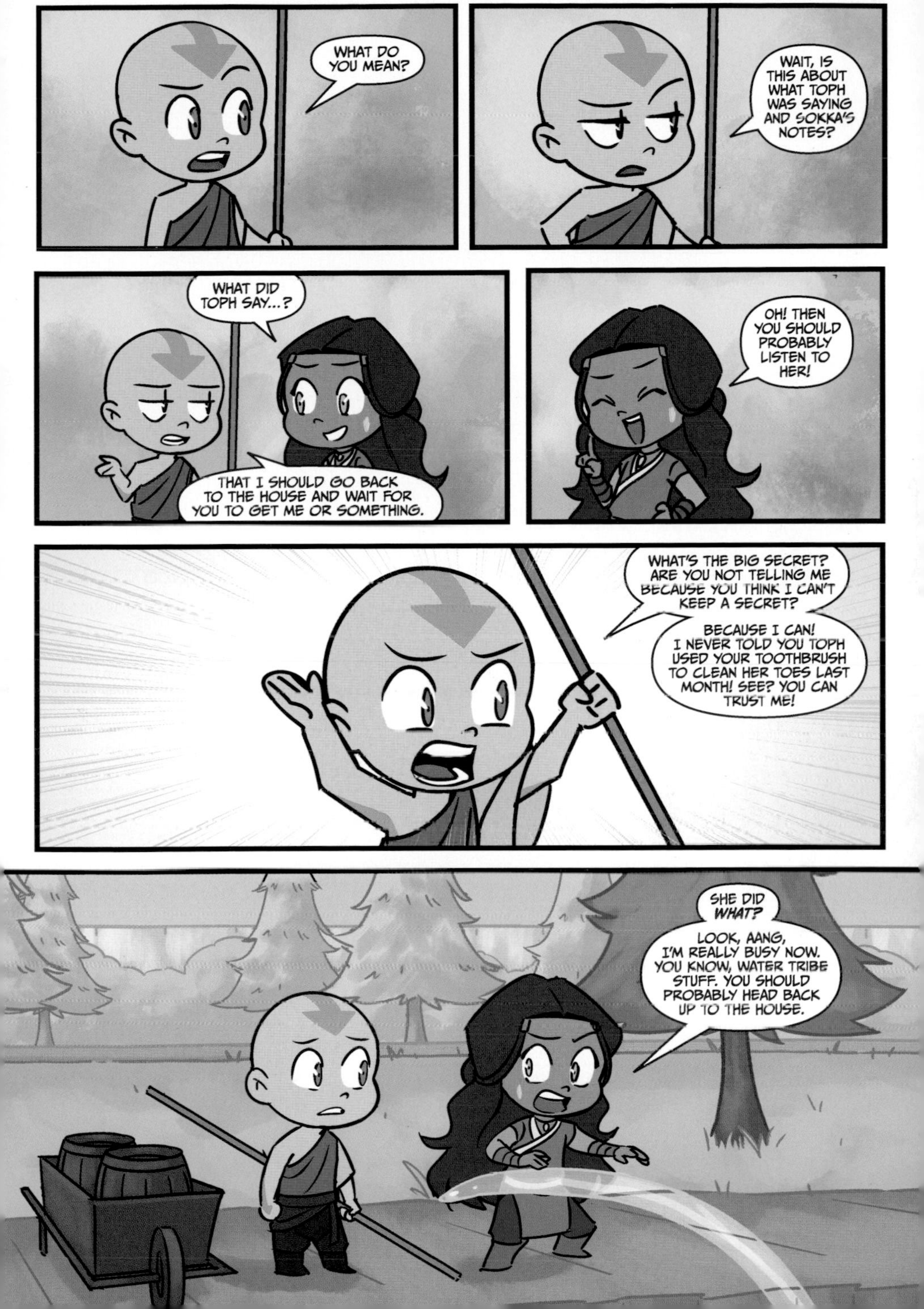
WHAT DO YOU MEAN?
WAIT, IS THIS ABOUT WHAT TOPH WAS SAYING AND SOKKA'S NOTES?
WHAT DID TOPH SAY...?
THAT I SHOULD GO BACK TO THE HOUSE AND WAIT FOR YOU TO GET ME OR SOMETHING.
OH! THEN YOU SHOULD PROBABLY LISTEN TO HER!
WHAT'S THE BIG SECRET? ARE YOU NOT TELLING ME BECAUSE YOU THINK I CAN'T KEEP A SECRET?
BECAUSE I CAN! I NEVER TOLD YOU TOPH USED YOUR TOOTHBRUSH TO CLEAN HER TOES LAST MONTH! SEE? YOU CAN TRUST ME!
SHE DID *WHAT?*
LOOK, AANG, I'M REALLY BUSY NOW. YOU KNOW, WATER TRIBE STUFF. YOU SHOULD PROBABLY HEAD BACK UP TO THE HOUSE.

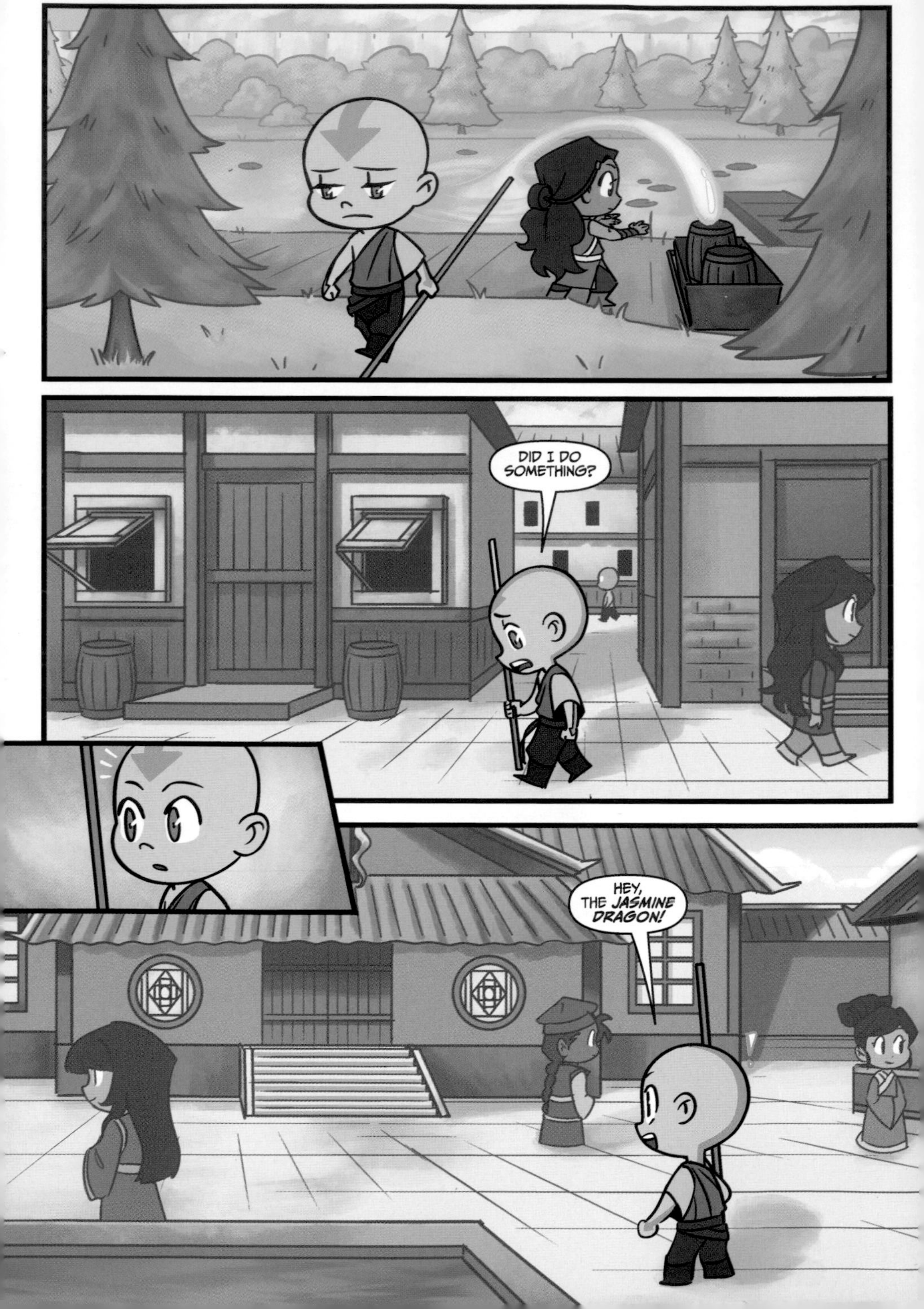
DID I DO SOMETHING?
HEY, THE JASMINE DRAGON!

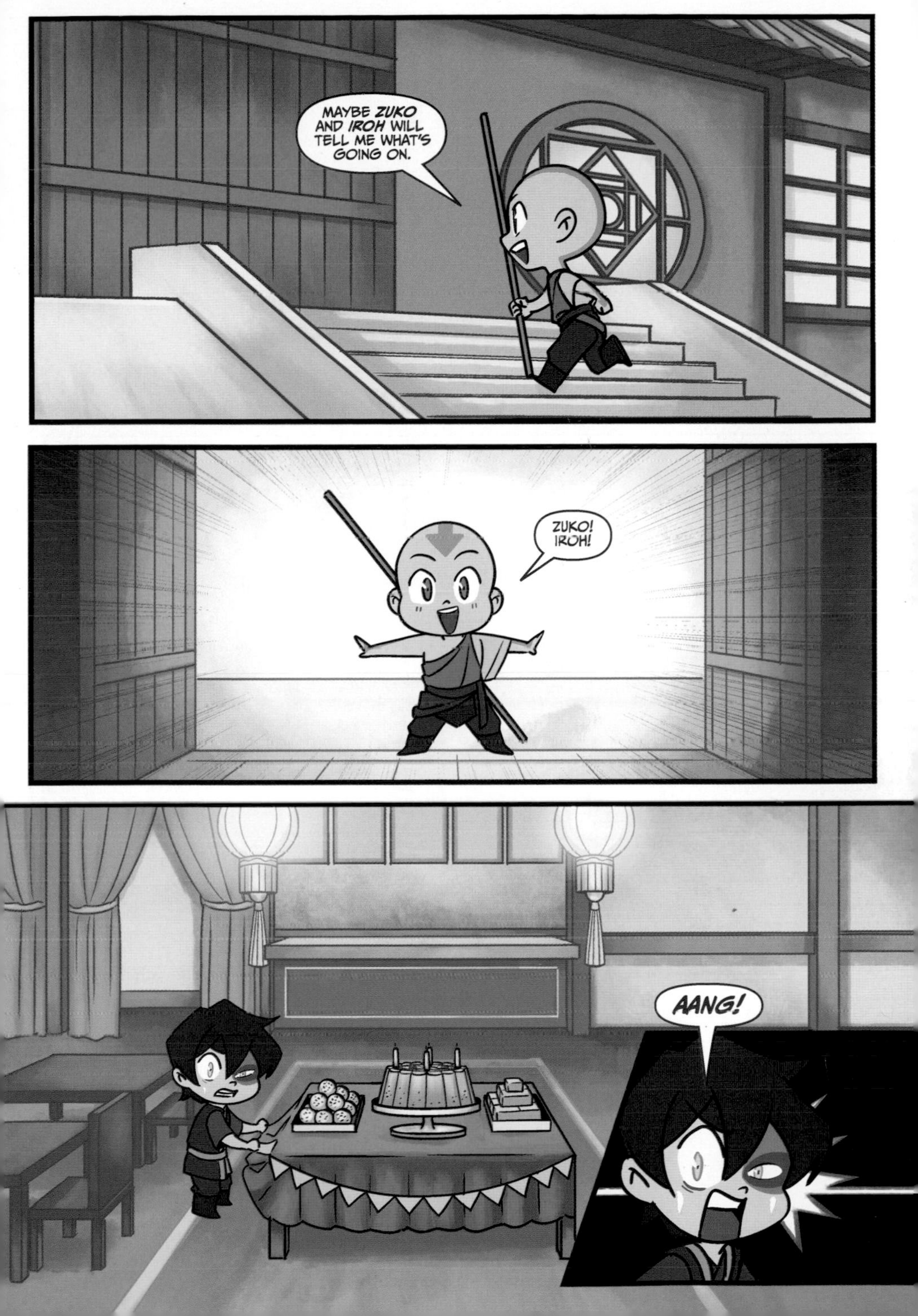
MAYBE *ZUKO* AND *IROH* WILL TELL ME WHAT'S GOING ON.
ZUKO! IROH!
*AANG!*

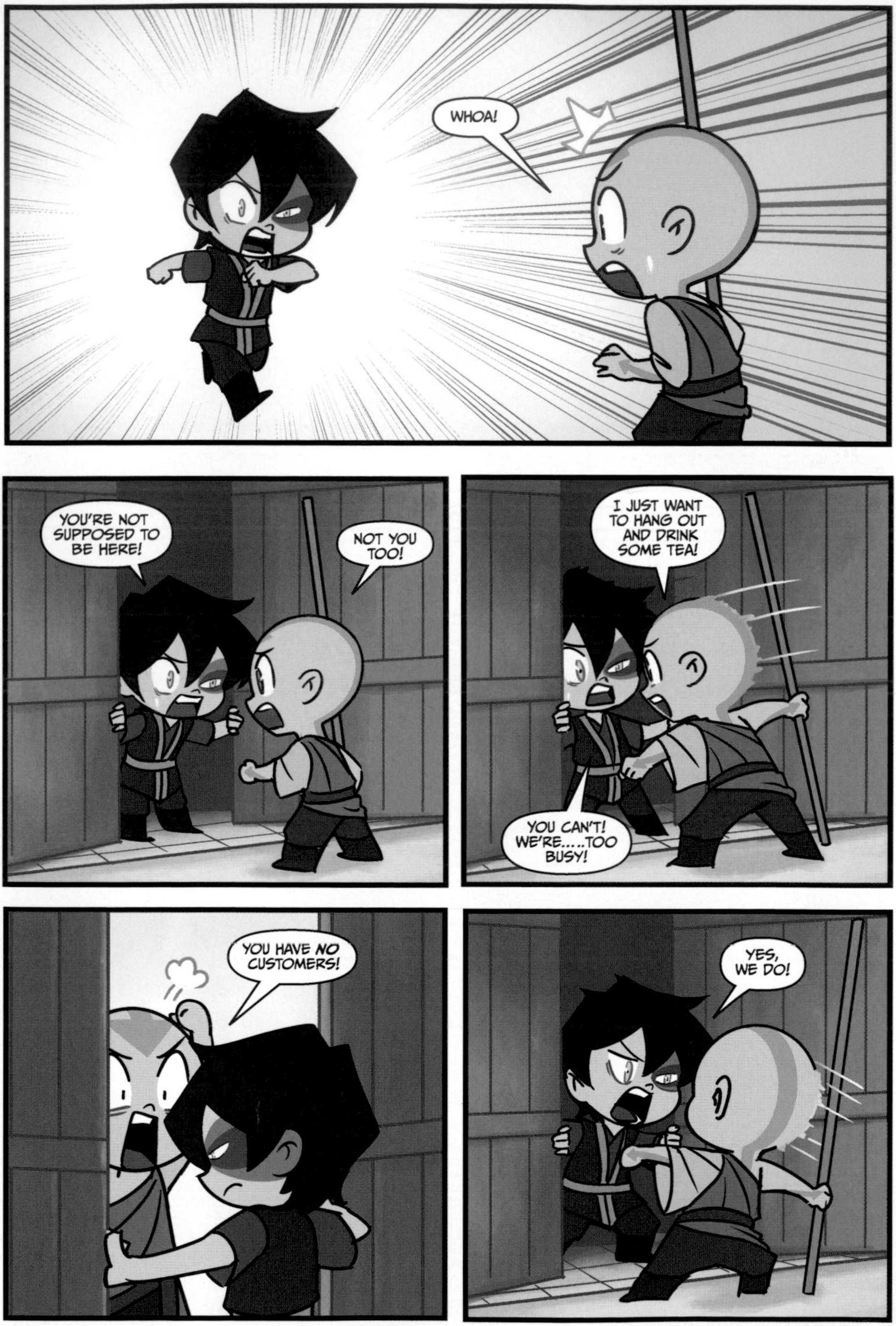
WHOA!
YOU'RE NOT SUPPOSED TO BE HERE!
NOT YOU TOO!
I JUST WANT TO HANG OUT AND DRINK SOME TEA!
YOU CAN'T! WE'RE.....TOO BUSY!
YOU HAVE NO CUSTOMERS!
YES, WE DO!

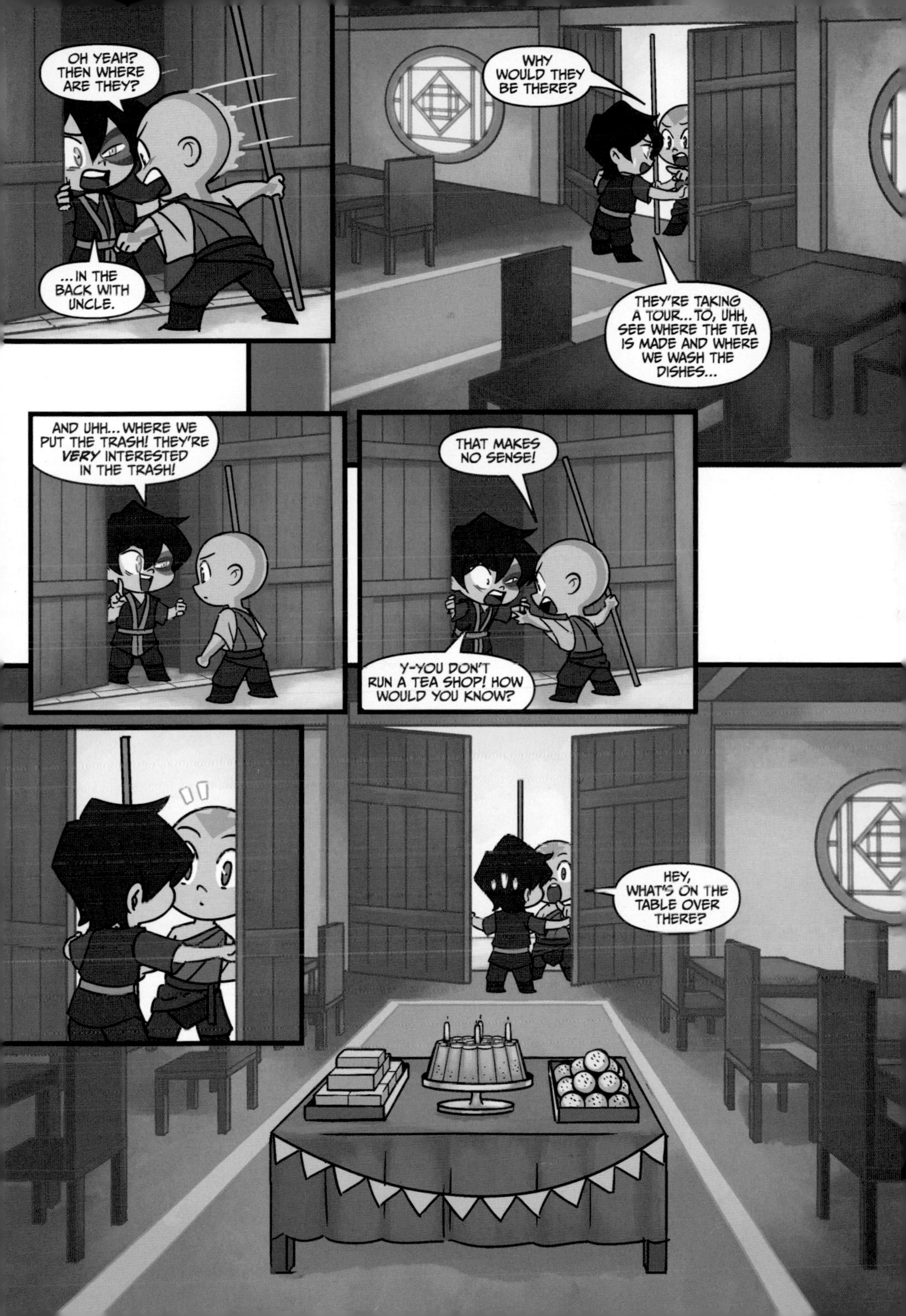
OH YEAH? THEN WHERE ARE THEY?
...IN THE BACK WITH UNCLE.
WHY WOULD THEY BE THERE?
THEY'RE TAKING A TOUR...TO, UHH, SEE WHERE THE TEA IS MADE AND WHERE WE WASH THE DISHES...
AND UHH...WHERE WE PUT THE TRASH! THEY'RE *VERY* INTERESTED IN THE TRASH!
THAT MAKES NO SENSE!
Y-YOU DON'T RUN A TEA SHOP! HOW WOULD YOU KNOW?
HEY, WHAT'S ON THE TABLE OVER THERE?

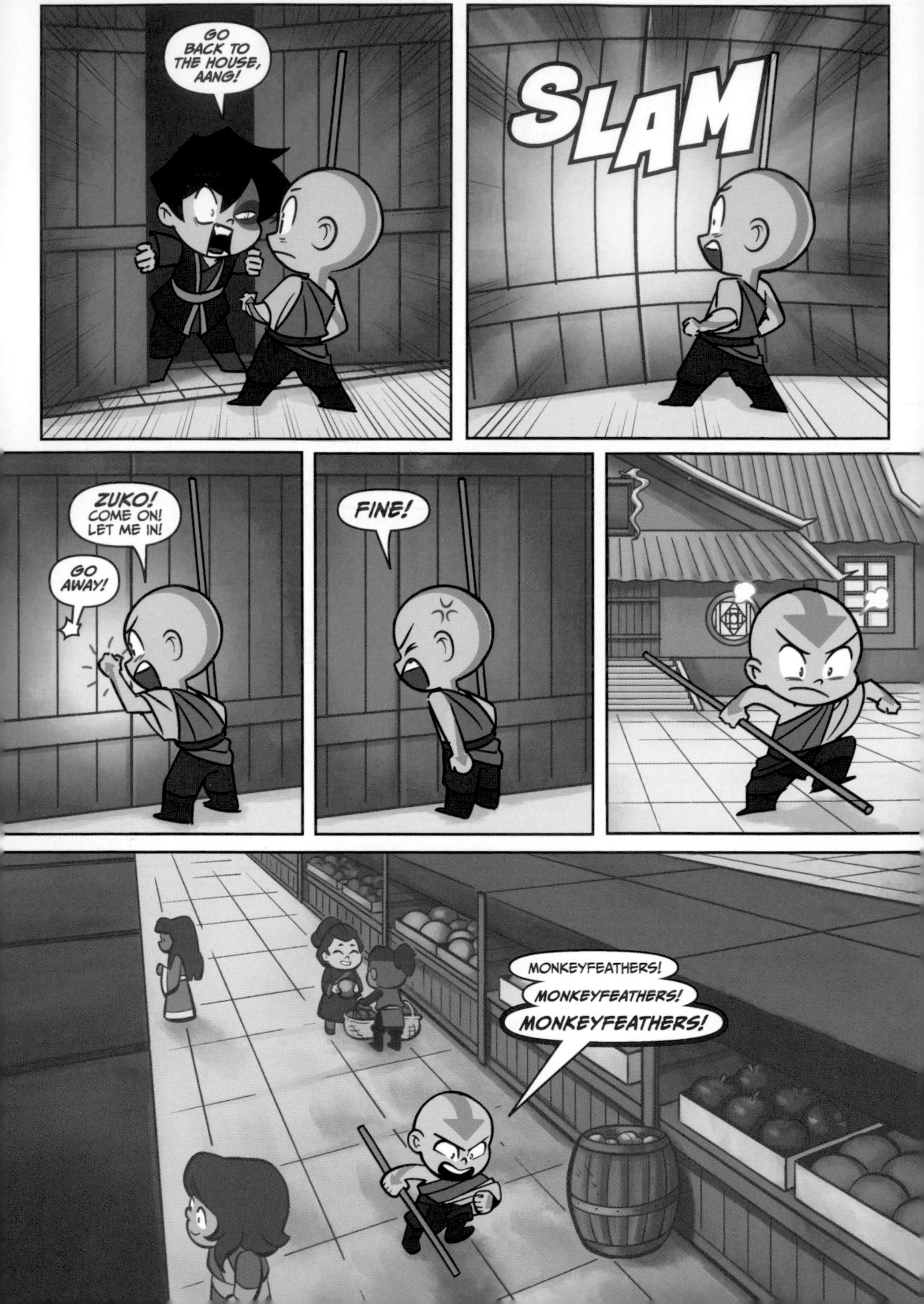
GO BACK TO THE HOUSE, AANG!
SLAM
ZUKO! COME ON! LET ME IN!
GO AWAY!
FINE!
MONKEYFEATHERS!
MONKEYFEATHERS!
MONKEYFEATHERS!

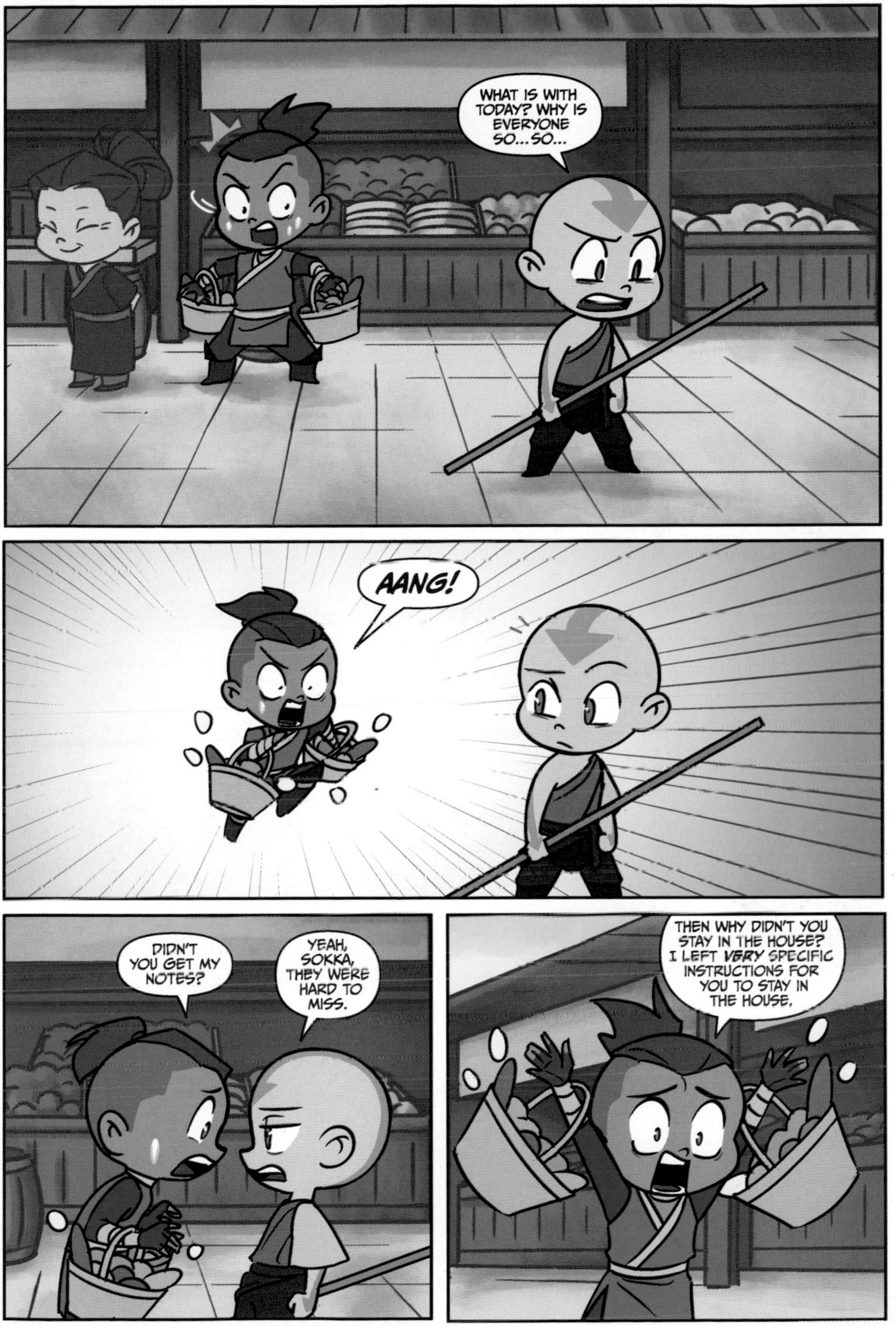
WHAT IS WITH TODAY? WHY IS EVERYONE SO... SO...
AANG!
DIDN'T YOU GET MY NOTES?
YEAH, SOKKA, THEY WERE HARD TO MISS.
THEN WHY DIDN'T YOU STAY IN THE HOUSE? I LEFT *VERY* SPECIFIC INSTRUCTIONS FOR YOU TO STAY IN THE HOUSE.

YEAH, I KNOW, BUT WHY?

UHH...

IS IT BECAUSE EVERYONE'S MAD AT ME?

WHAT? MAD? WE'RE NOT MAD. WHY DO YOU THINK WE'RE MAD?

WELL, BOTH TOPH AND KATARA ACTED LIKE I WAS BOTHERING THEM WHEN I TRIED TO HANG OUT.

UH, YOU KNOW THEM...PROBABLY JUST BUSY WITH THEIR *BENDING* STUFF.

THEN ZUKO KICKED ME OUT OF THE JASMINE DRAGON AND I HAVE NO IDEA WHY!

ZUKO'S ALWAYS MAD. WHO CAN KEEP TRACK OF WHAT HE'S MAD ABOUT THIS TIME?

I GUESS... HEY, WHAT'S ALL THAT FOOD FOR?

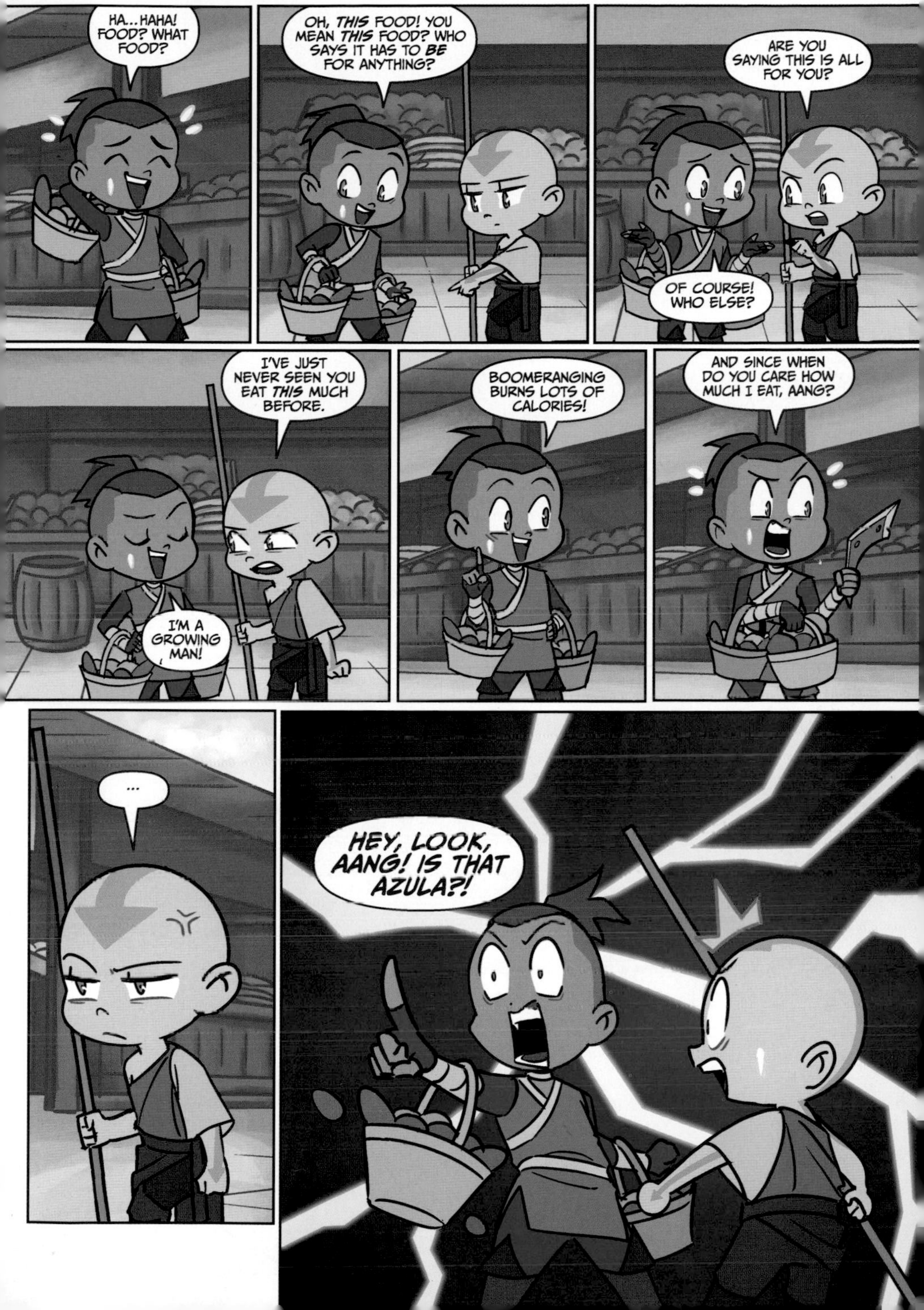
HA...HAHA! FOOD? WHAT FOOD?
OH, THIS FOOD! YOU MEAN THIS FOOD? WHO SAYS IT HAS TO BE FOR ANYTHING?
ARE YOU SAYING THIS IS ALL FOR YOU?
OF COURSE! WHO ELSE?
I'VE JUST NEVER SEEN YOU EAT THIS MUCH BEFORE.
I'M A GROWING MAN!
BOOMERANGING BURNS LOTS OF CALORIES!
AND SINCE WHEN DO YOU CARE HOW MUCH I EAT, AANG?
...
HEY, LOOK, AANG! IS THAT AZULA?!

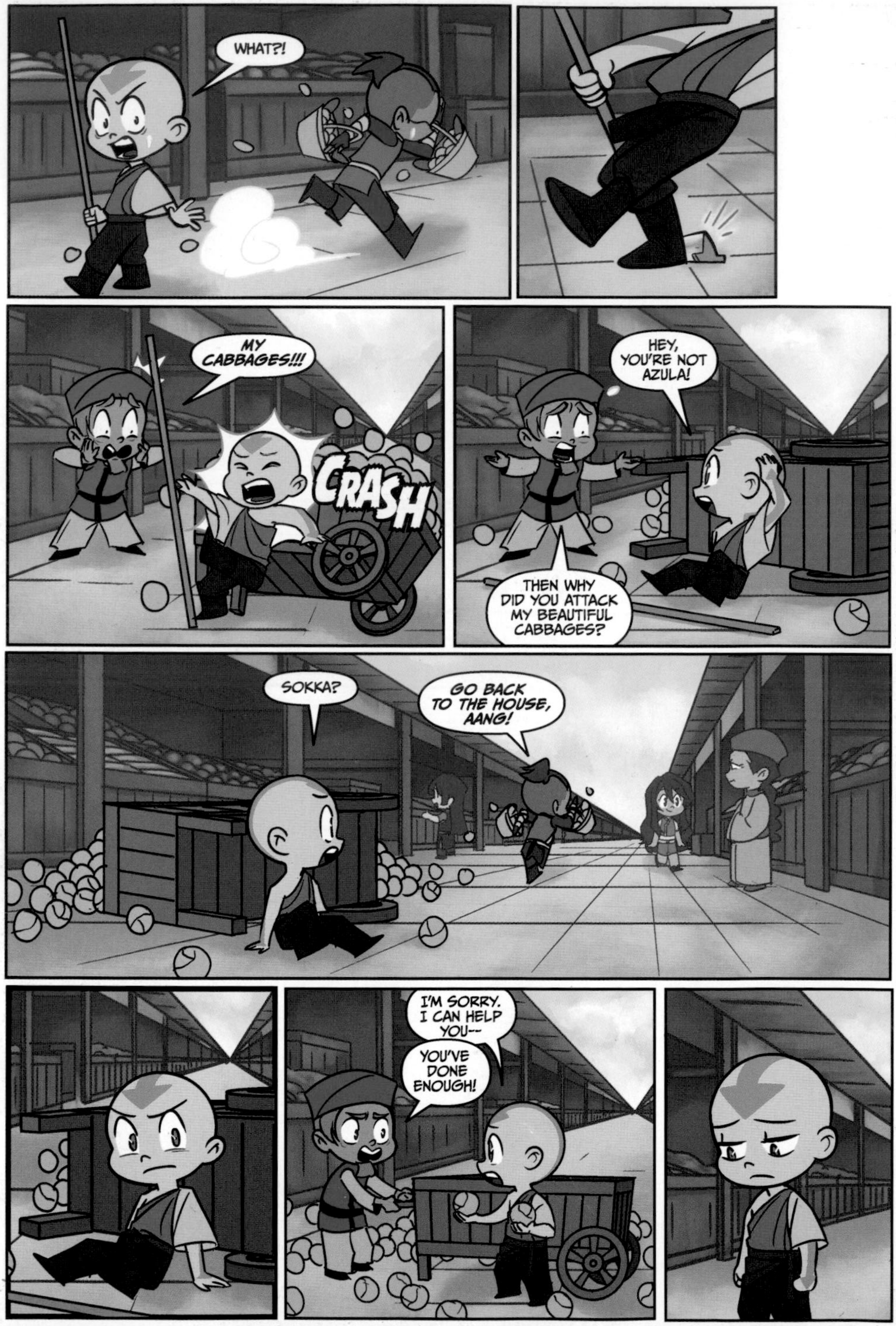
WHAT?!
MY CABBAGES!!!
CRASH
HEY, YOU'RE NOT AZULA!
THEN WHY DID YOU ATTACK MY BEAUTIFUL CABBAGES?
SOKKA?
GO BACK TO THE HOUSE, AANG!
I'M SORRY. I CAN HELP YOU--
YOU'VE DONE ENOUGH!

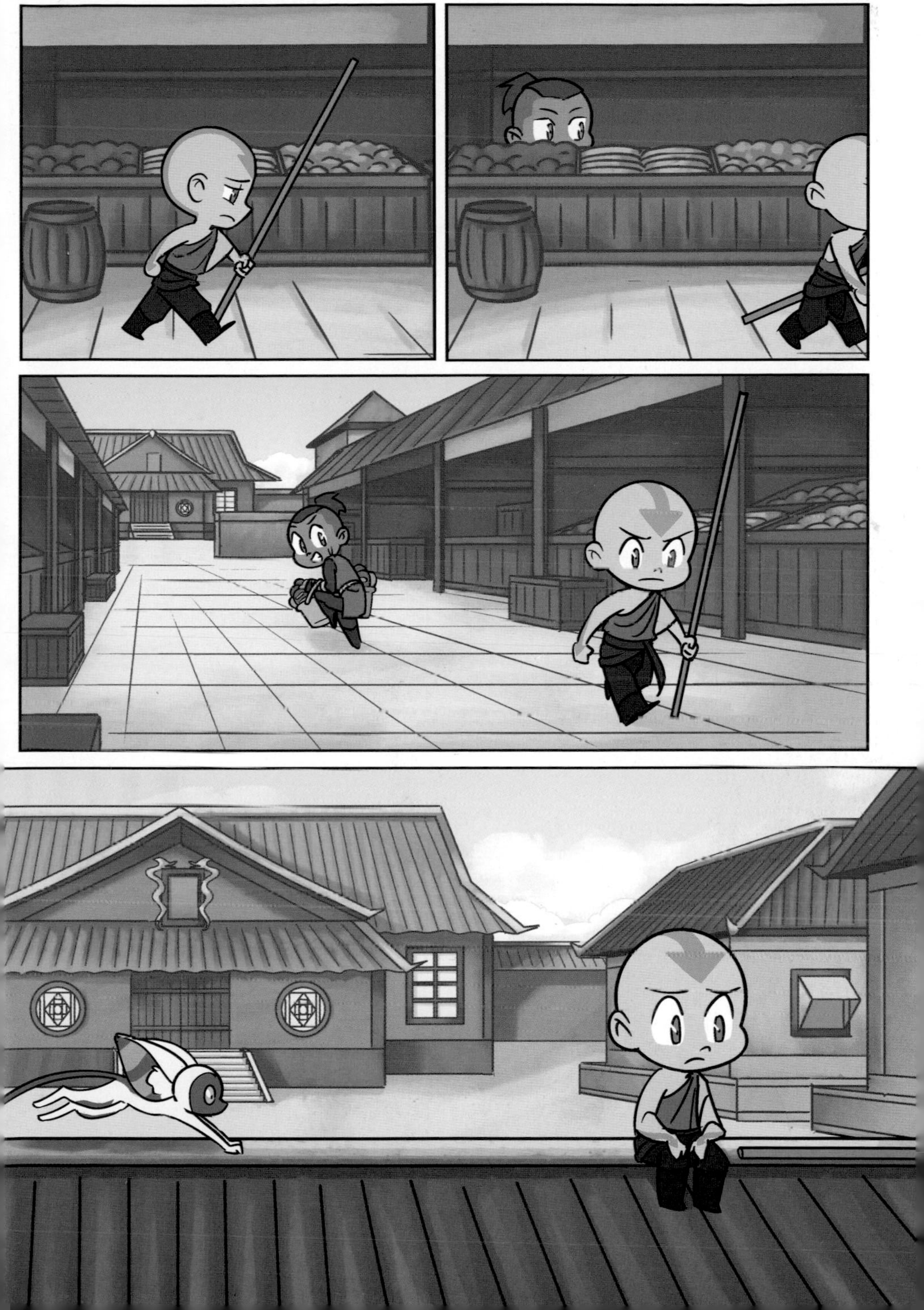

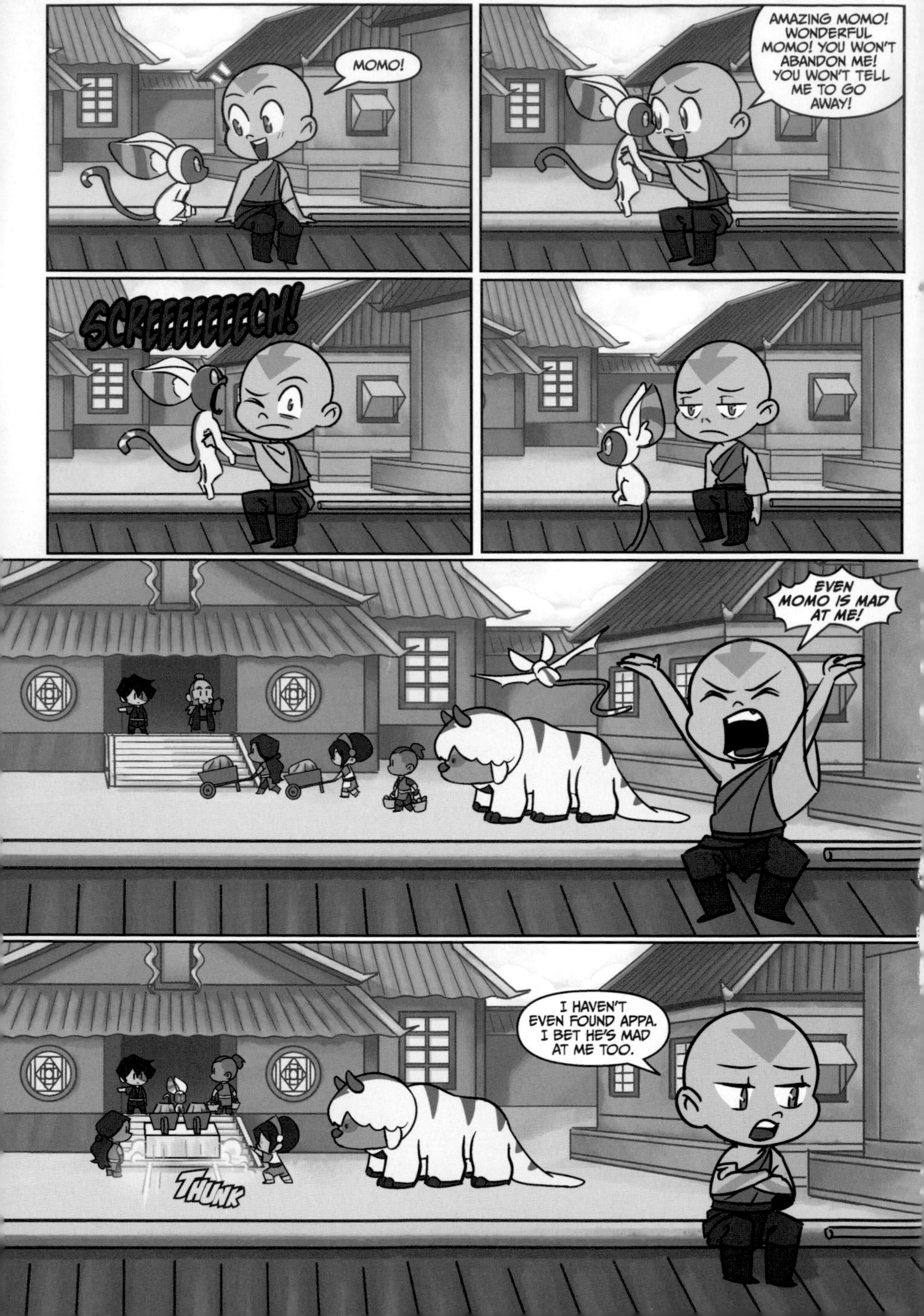
MOMO!
AMAZING MOMO! WONDERFUL MOMO! YOU WON'T ABANDON ME! YOU WON'T TELL ME TO GO AWAY!
SCREEEEEEEEECH!
EVEN MOMO IS MAD AT ME!
I HAVEN'T EVEN FOUND APPA. I BET HE'S MAD AT ME TOO.
THUNK

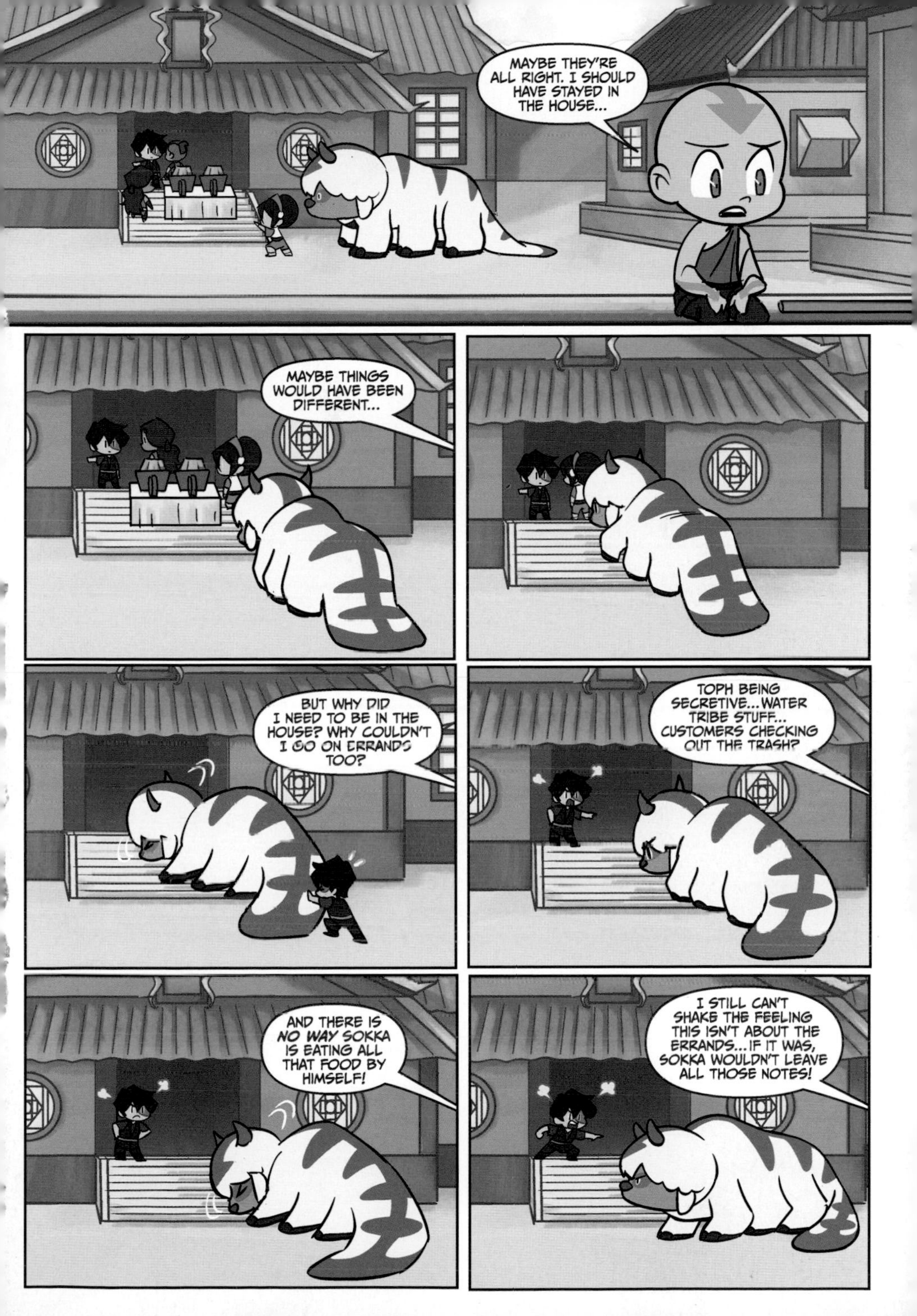

MAYBE THEY'RE ALL RIGHT. I SHOULD HAVE STAYED IN THE HOUSE...
MAYBE THINGS WOULD HAVE BEEN DIFFERENT...
BUT WHY DID I NEED TO BE IN THE HOUSE? WHY COULDN'T I GO ON ERRANDS TOO?
TOPH BEING SECRETIVE...WATER TRIBE STUFF... CUSTOMERS CHECKING OUT THE TRASH?
AND THERE IS *NO WAY* SOKKA IS EATING ALL THAT FOOD BY HIMSELF!
I STILL CAN'T SHAKE THE FEELING THIS ISN'T ABOUT THE ERRANDS...IF IT WAS, SOKKA WOULDN'T LEAVE ALL THOSE NOTES!

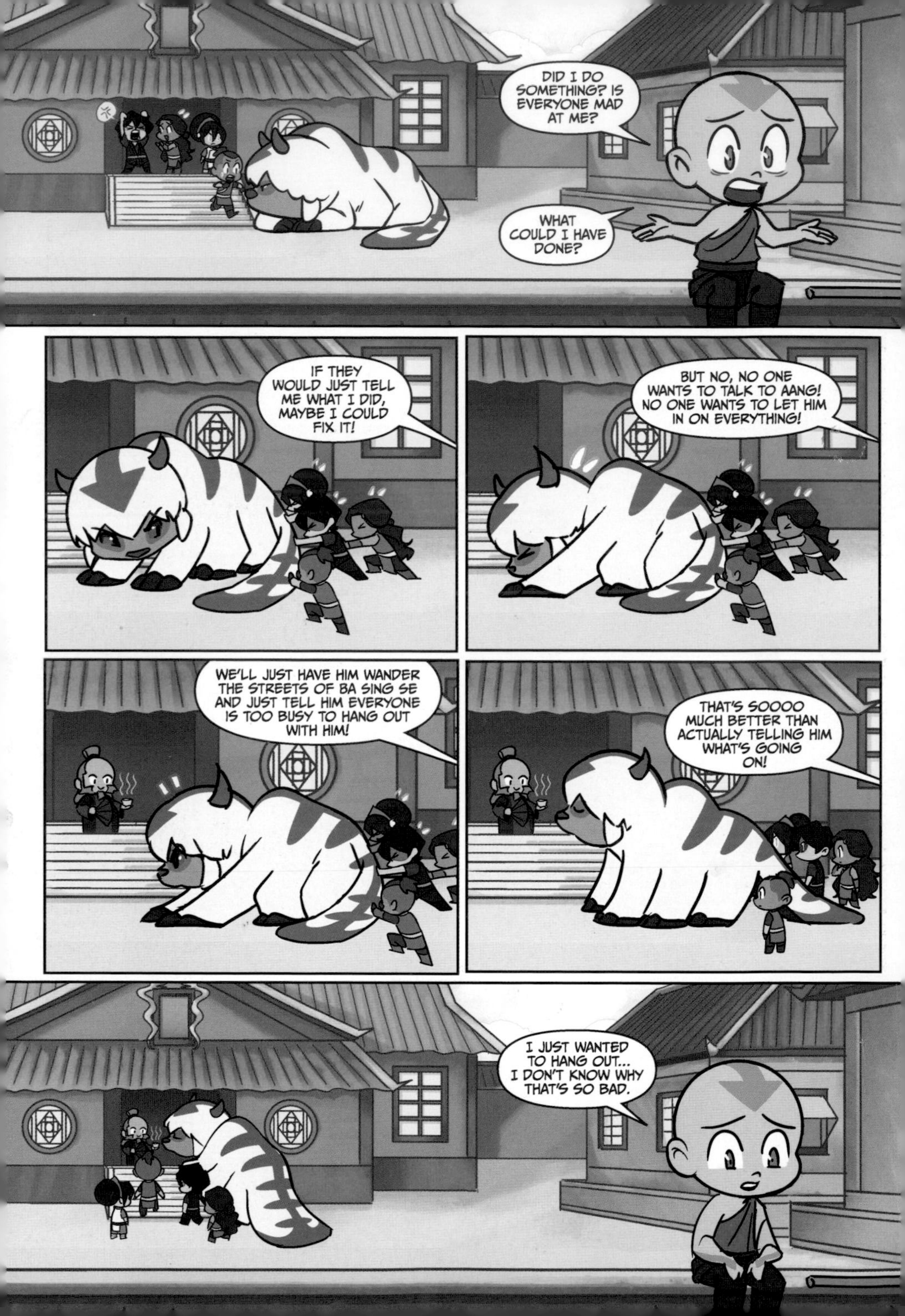

DID I DO SOMETHING? IS EVERYONE MAD AT ME?
WHAT COULD I HAVE DONE?
IF THEY WOULD JUST TELL ME WHAT I DID, MAYBE I COULD FIX IT!
BUT NO, NO ONE WANTS TO TALK TO AANG! NO ONE WANTS TO LET HIM IN ON EVERYTHING!
WE'LL JUST HAVE HIM WANDER THE STREETS OF BA SING SE AND JUST TELL HIM EVERYONE IS TOO BUSY TO HANG OUT WITH HIM!
THAT'S SOOOO MUCH BETTER THAN ACTUALLY TELLING HIM WHAT'S GOING ON!
I JUST WANTED TO HANG OUT... I DON'T KNOW WHY THAT'S SO BAD.

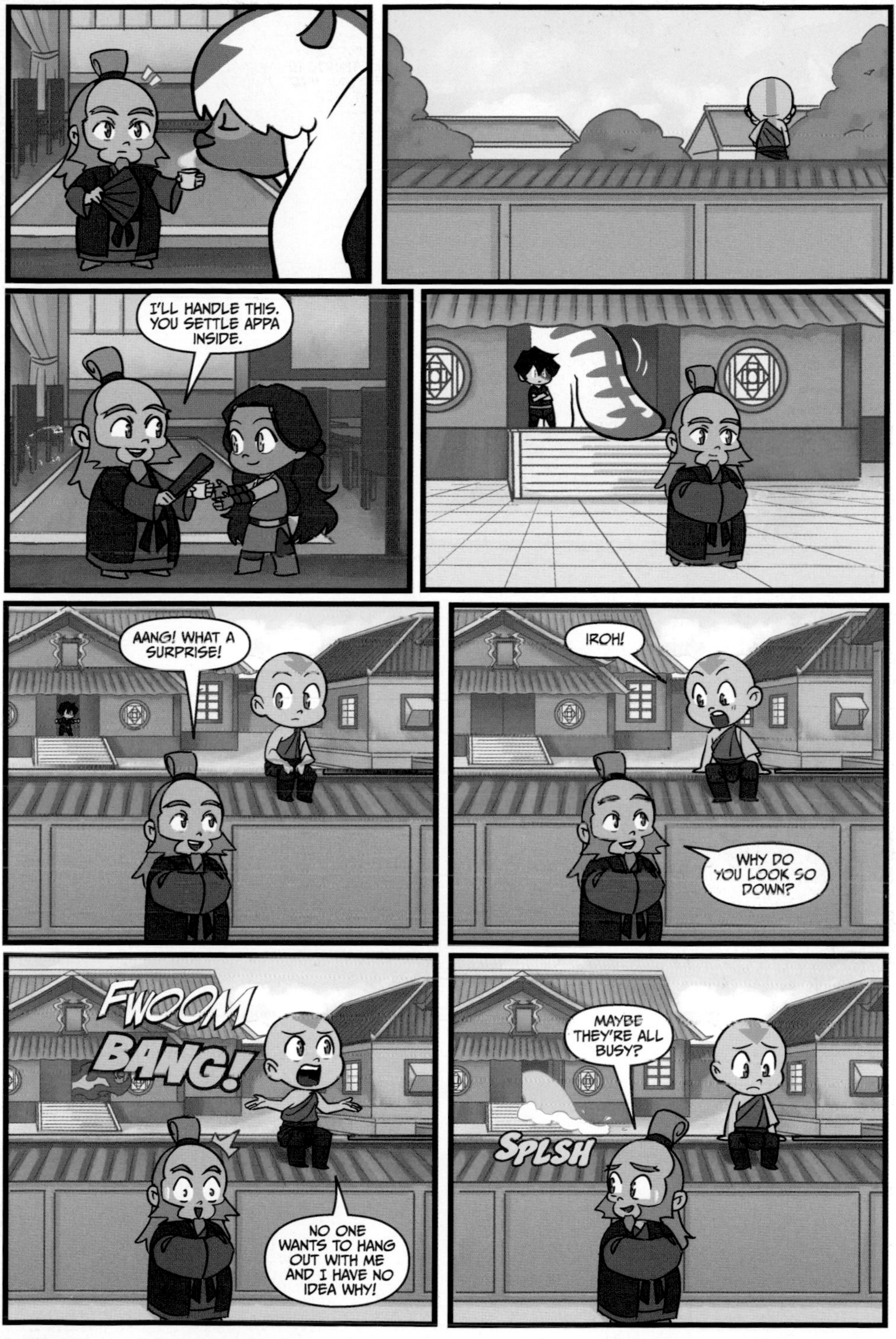
I'LL HANDLE THIS. YOU SETTLE APPA INSIDE.
AANG! WHAT A SURPRISE!
IROH!
WHY DO YOU LOOK SO DOWN?
FWOOM
BANG!
NO ONE WANTS TO HANG OUT WITH ME AND I HAVE NO IDEA WHY!
MAYBE THEY'RE ALL BUSY?
SPLSH

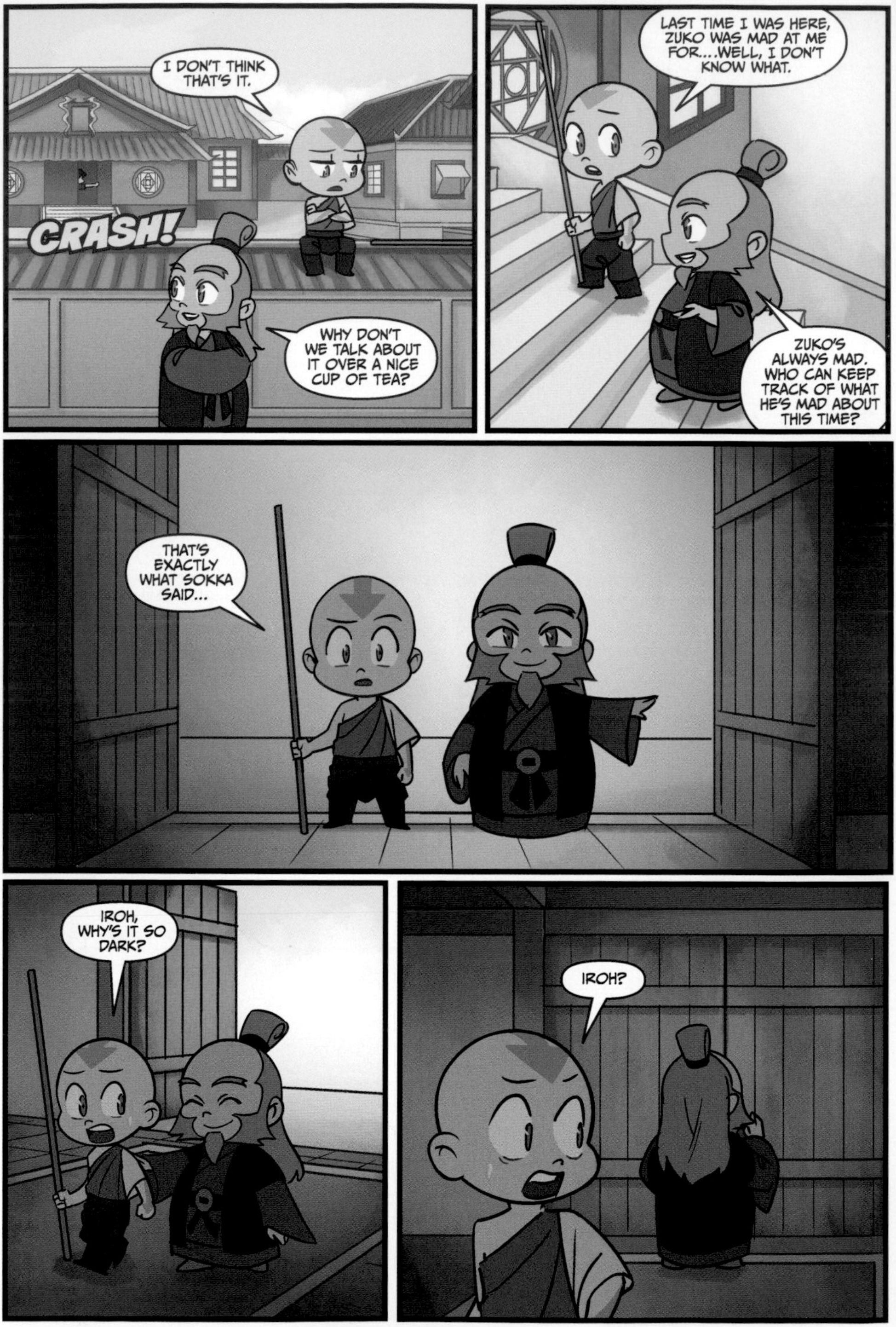
I DON'T THINK THAT'S IT.
CRASH!
WHY DON'T WE TALK ABOUT IT OVER A NICE CUP OF TEA?
LAST TIME I WAS HERE, ZUKO WAS MAD AT ME FOR....WELL, I DON'T KNOW WHAT.
ZUKO'S ALWAYS MAD. WHO CAN KEEP TRACK OF WHAT HE'S MAD ABOUT THIS TIME?
THAT'S EXACTLY WHAT SOKKA SAID...
IROH, WHY'S IT SO DARK?
IROH?

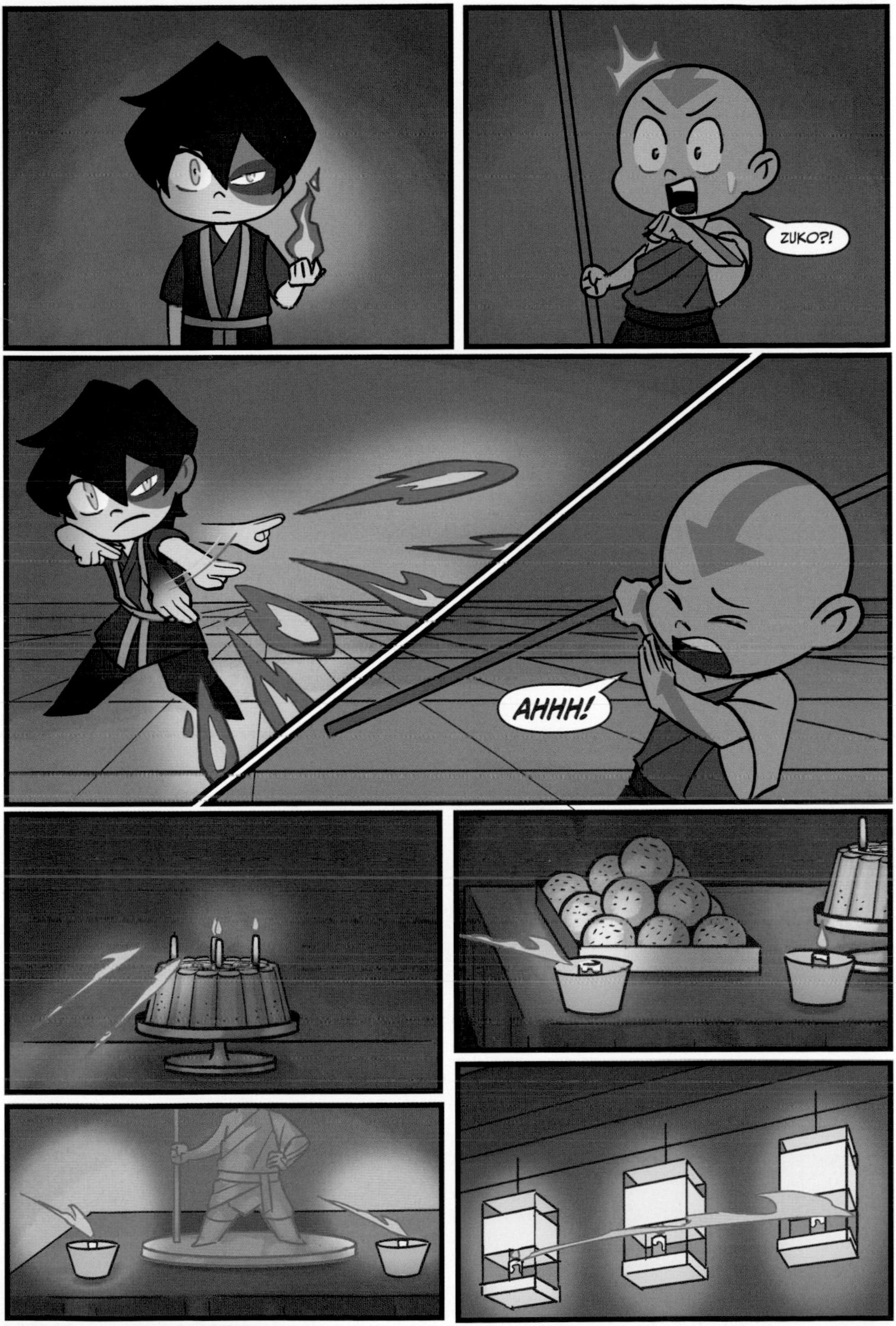
ZUKO?!
AHHH!

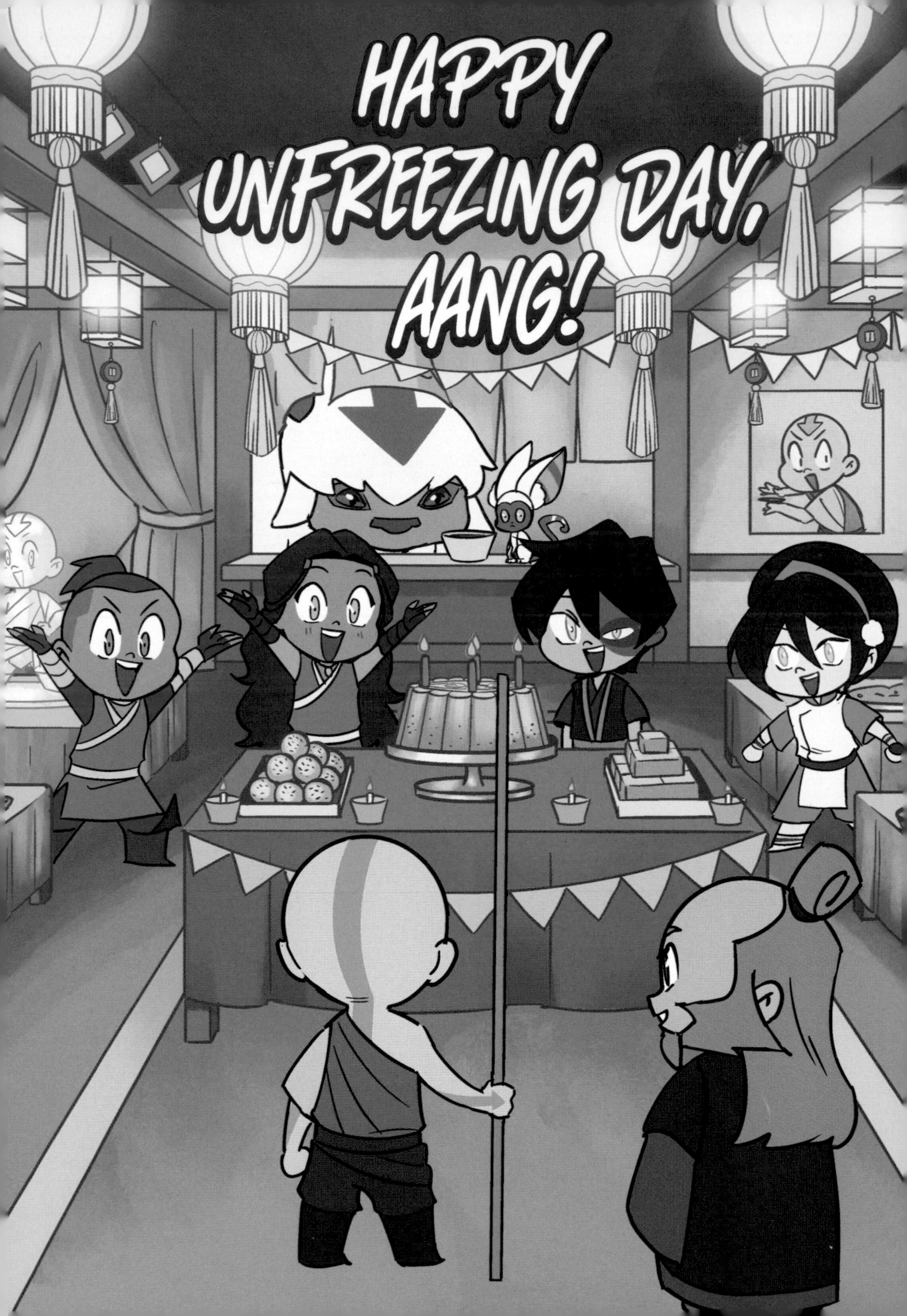
HAPPY UNFREEZING DAY, AANG!

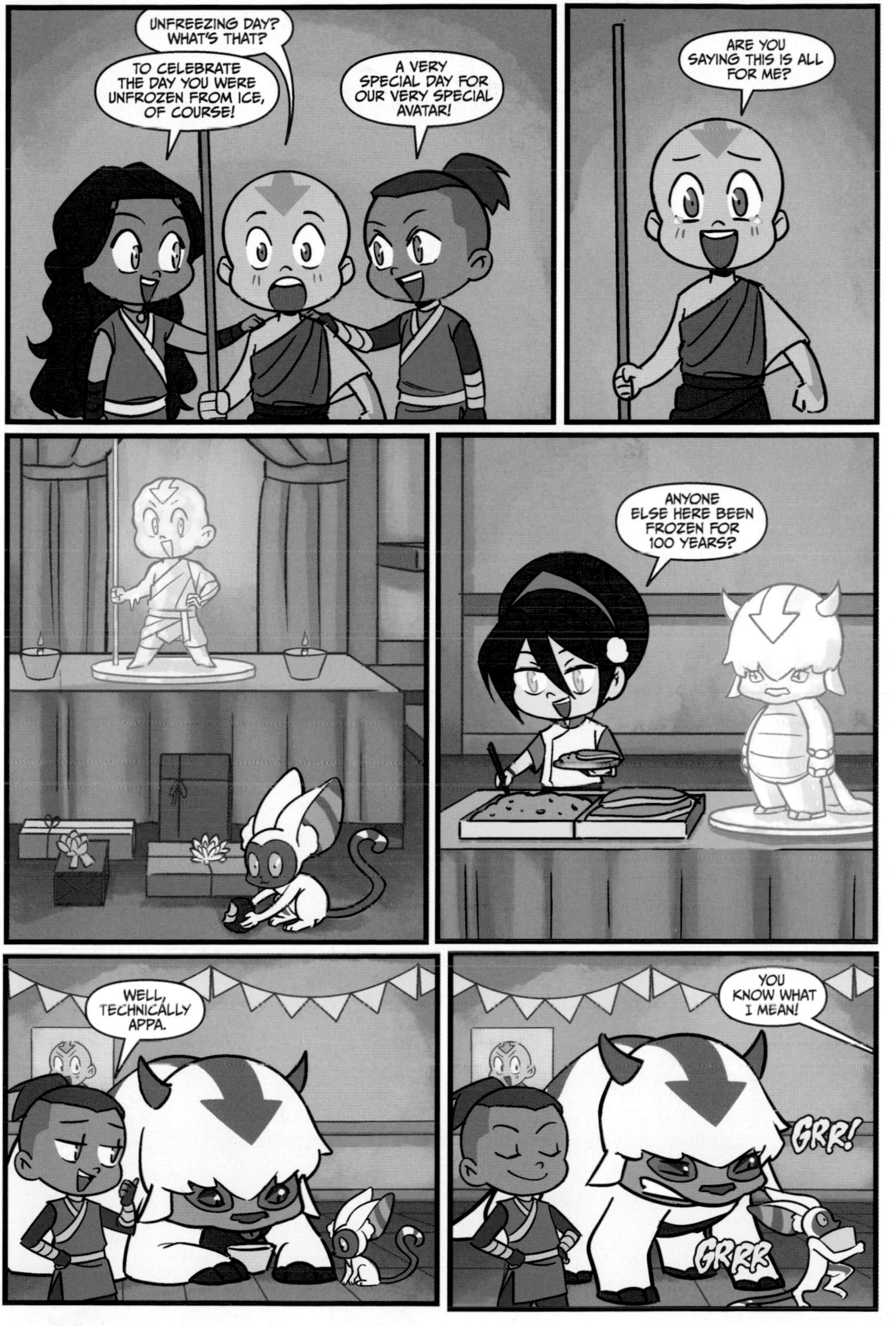
UNFREEZING DAY? WHAT'S THAT?
TO CELEBRATE THE DAY YOU WERE UNFROZEN FROM ICE, OF COURSE!
A VERY SPECIAL DAY FOR OUR VERY SPECIAL AVATAR!
ARE YOU SAYING THIS IS ALL FOR ME?
ANYONE ELSE HERE BEEN FROZEN FOR 100 YEARS?
WELL, TECHNICALLY APPA.
YOU KNOW WHAT I MEAN!
GRR!
GRRR

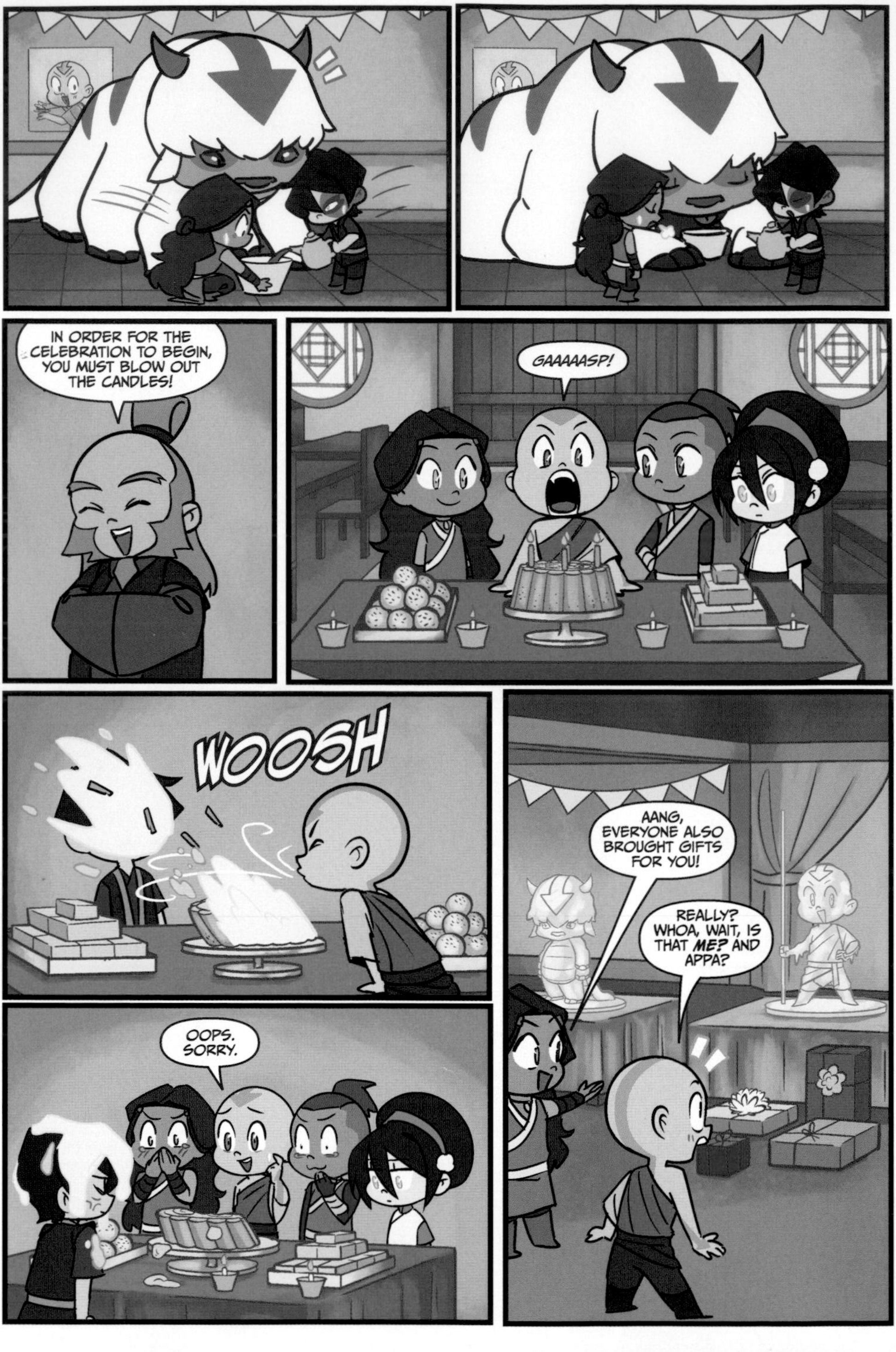
IN ORDER FOR THE CELEBRATION TO BEGIN, YOU MUST BLOW OUT THE CANDLES!
GAAAAASP!
WOOSH
OOPS. SORRY.
AANG, EVERYONE ALSO BROUGHT GIFTS FOR YOU!
REALLY? WHOA, WAIT, IS THAT *ME?* AND APPA?

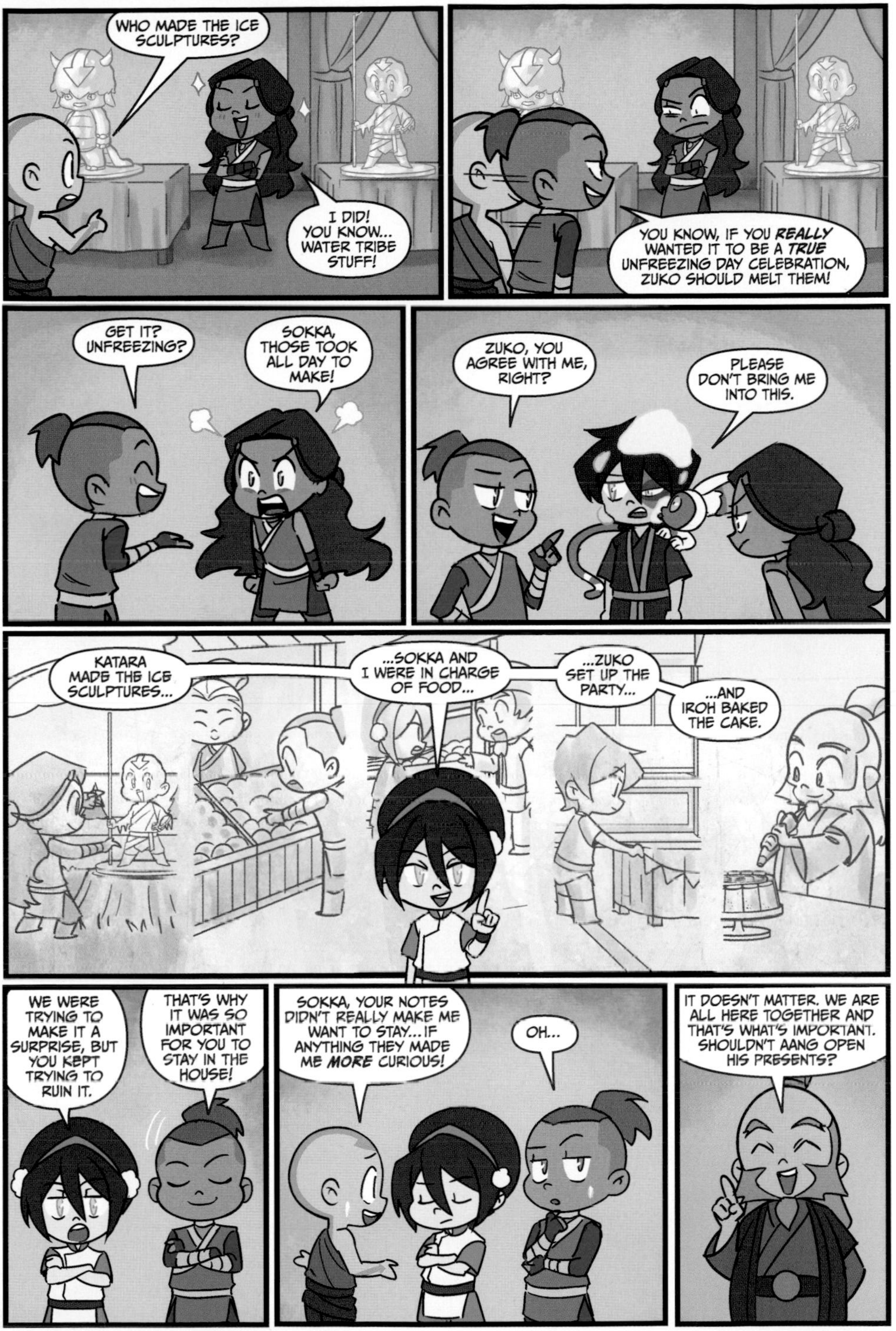
WHO MADE THE ICE SCULPTURES?
I DID! YOU KNOW... WATER TRIBE STUFF!
YOU KNOW, IF YOU **REALLY** WANTED IT TO BE A **TRUE** UNFREEZING DAY CELEBRATION, ZUKO SHOULD MELT THEM!
GET IT? UNFREEZING?
SOKKA, THOSE TOOK ALL DAY TO MAKE!
ZUKO, YOU AGREE WITH ME, RIGHT?
PLEASE DON'T BRING ME INTO THIS.
KATARA MADE THE ICE SCULPTURES...
...SOKKA AND I WERE IN CHARGE OF FOOD...
...ZUKO SET UP THE PARTY...
...AND IROH BAKED THE CAKE.
WE WERE TRYING TO MAKE IT A SURPRISE, BUT YOU KEPT TRYING TO RUIN IT.
THAT'S WHY IT WAS SO IMPORTANT FOR YOU TO STAY IN THE HOUSE!
SOKKA, YOUR NOTES DIDN'T REALLY MAKE ME WANT TO STAY... IF ANYTHING THEY MADE ME **MORE** CURIOUS!
OH...
IT DOESN'T MATTER. WE ARE ALL HERE TOGETHER AND THAT'S WHAT'S IMPORTANT. SHOULDN'T AANG OPEN HIS PRESENTS?

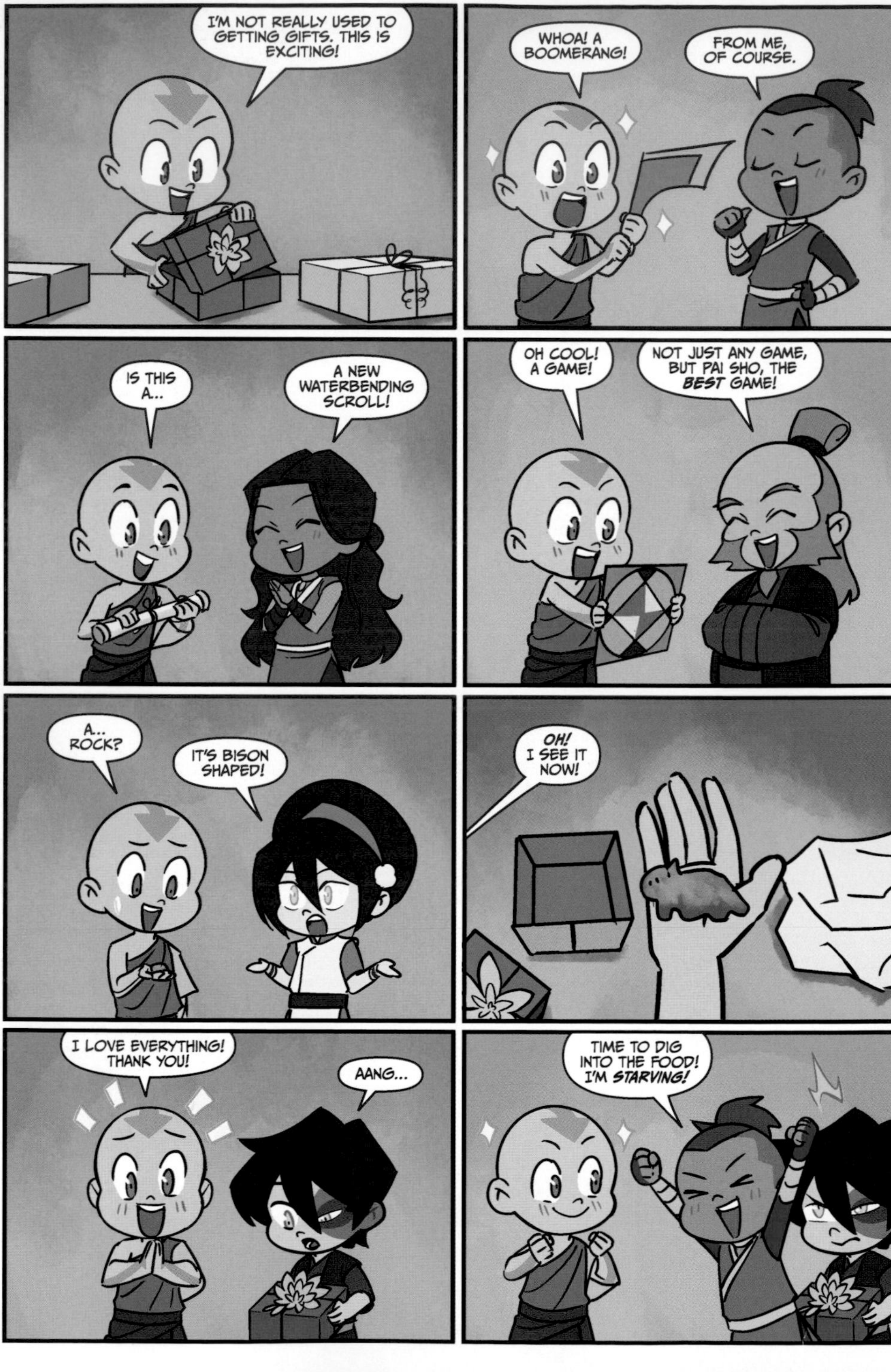

I'M NOT REALLY USED TO GETTING GIFTS. THIS IS EXCITING!
WHOA! A BOOMERANG!
FROM ME, OF COURSE.
IS THIS A...
A NEW WATERBENDING SCROLL!
OH COOL! A GAME!
NOT JUST ANY GAME, BUT PAI SHO, THE BEST GAME!
A... ROCK?
IT'S BISON SHAPED!
OH! I SEE IT NOW!
I LOVE EVERYTHING! THANK YOU!
AANG...
TIME TO DIG INTO THE FOOD! I'M STARVING!

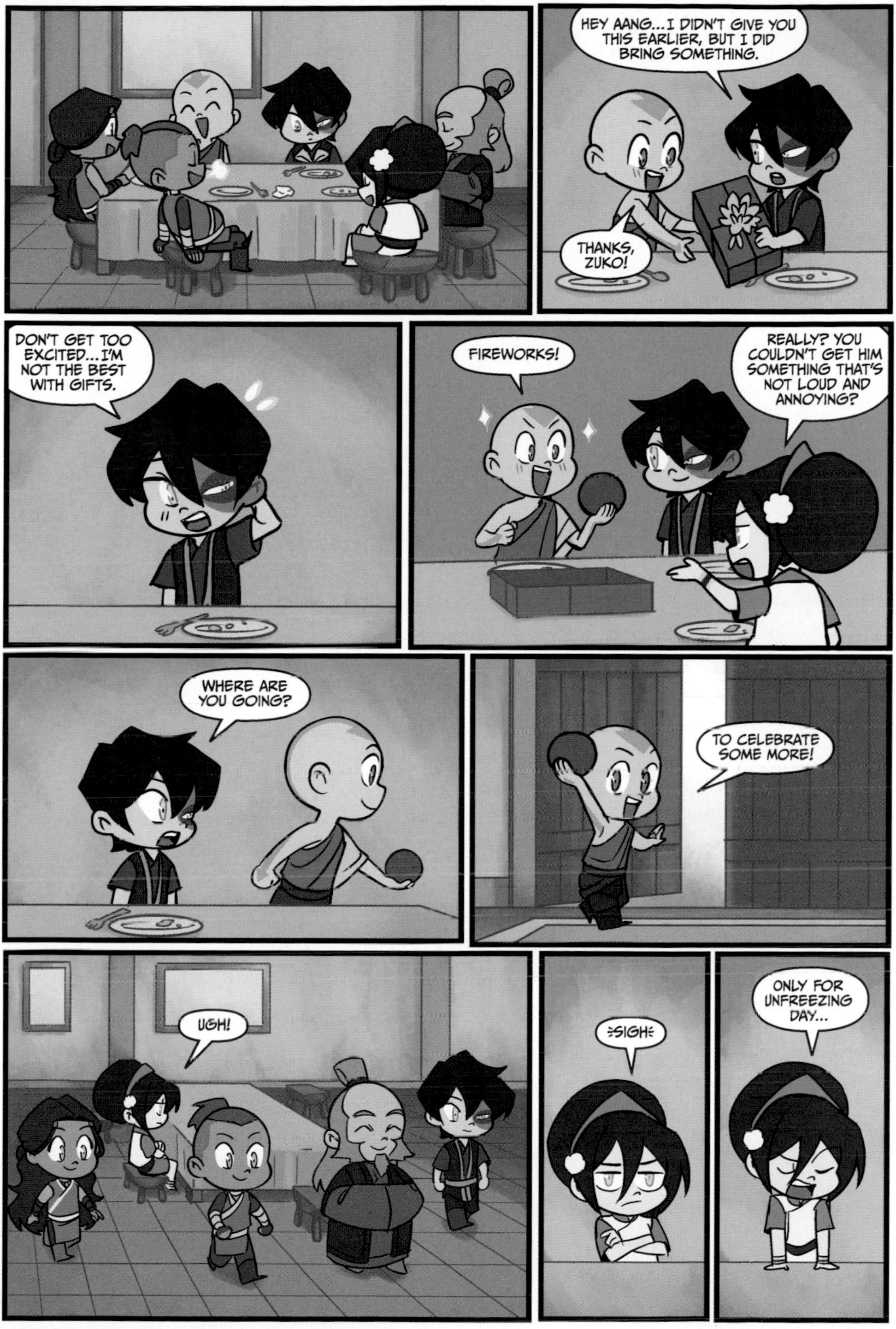
HEY AANG...I DIDN'T GIVE YOU THIS EARLIER, BUT I DID BRING SOMETHING.
THANKS, ZUKO!
DON'T GET TOO EXCITED...I'M NOT THE BEST WITH GIFTS.
FIREWORKS!
REALLY? YOU COULDN'T GET HIM SOMETHING THAT'S NOT LOUD AND ANNOYING?
WHERE ARE YOU GOING?
TO CELEBRATE SOME MORE!
UGH!
SIGH
ONLY FOR UNFREEZING DAY...

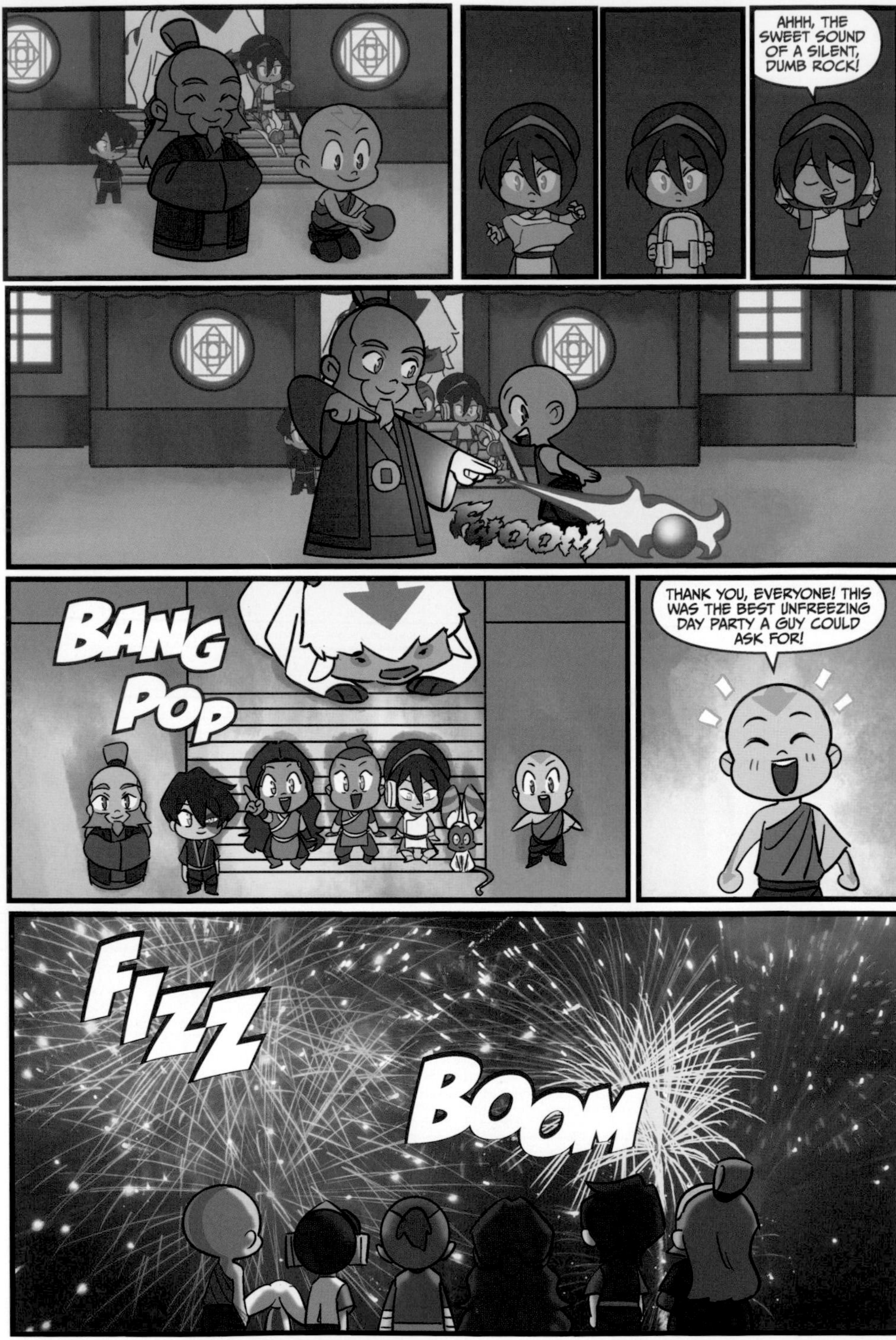
AHHH, THE SWEET SOUND OF A SILENT, DUMB ROCK!
FWOOM
BANG
POP
THANK YOU, EVERYONE! THIS WAS THE BEST UNFREEZING DAY PARTY A GUY COULD ASK FOR!
FIZZ
BOOM

# HOW TO MAKE COMICS!

Before the artist starts drawing the comic, they do some sketches of the characters to make sure they have the design juuuuuuuust right! This practice usually happens while the writer is writing the script.

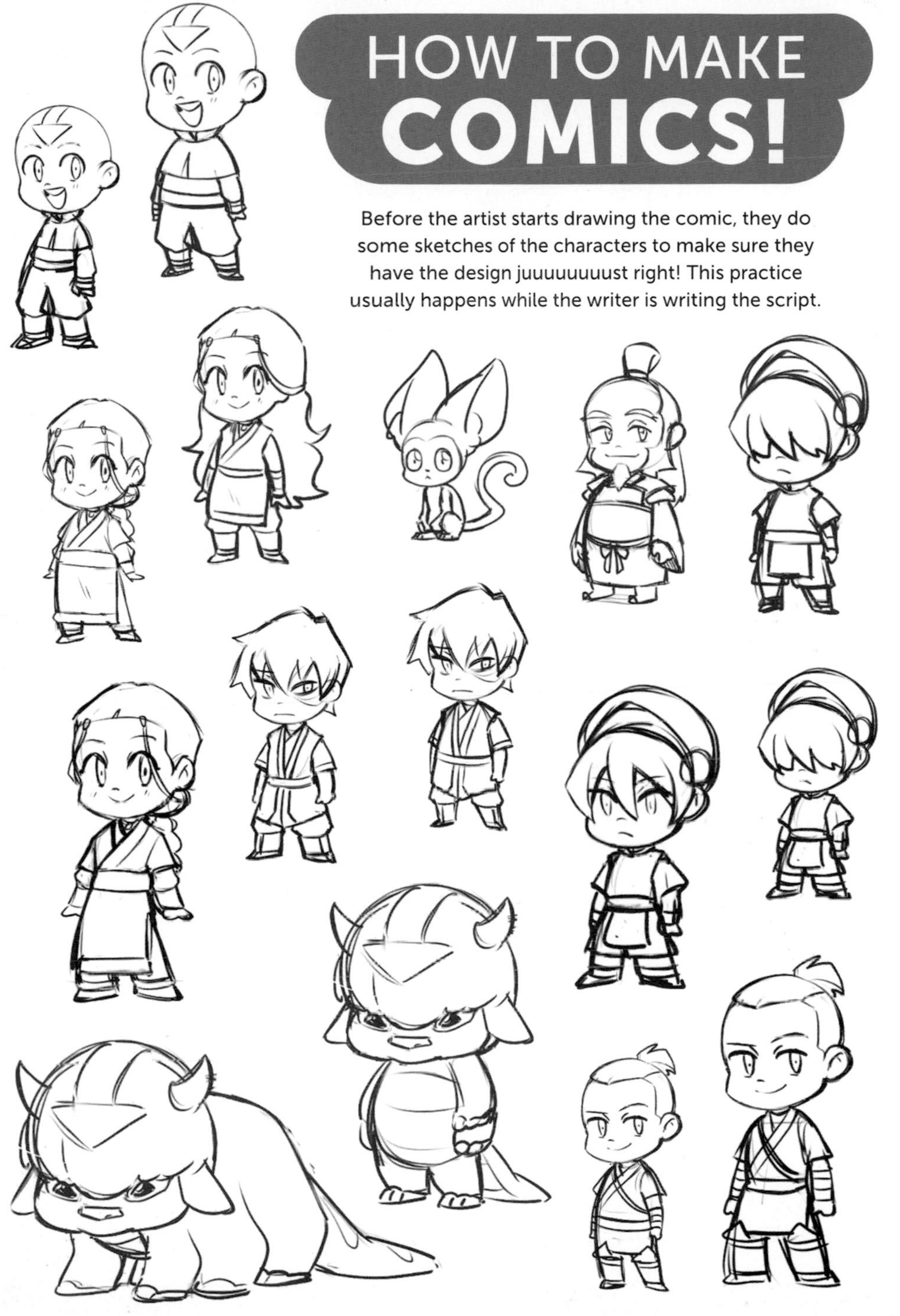

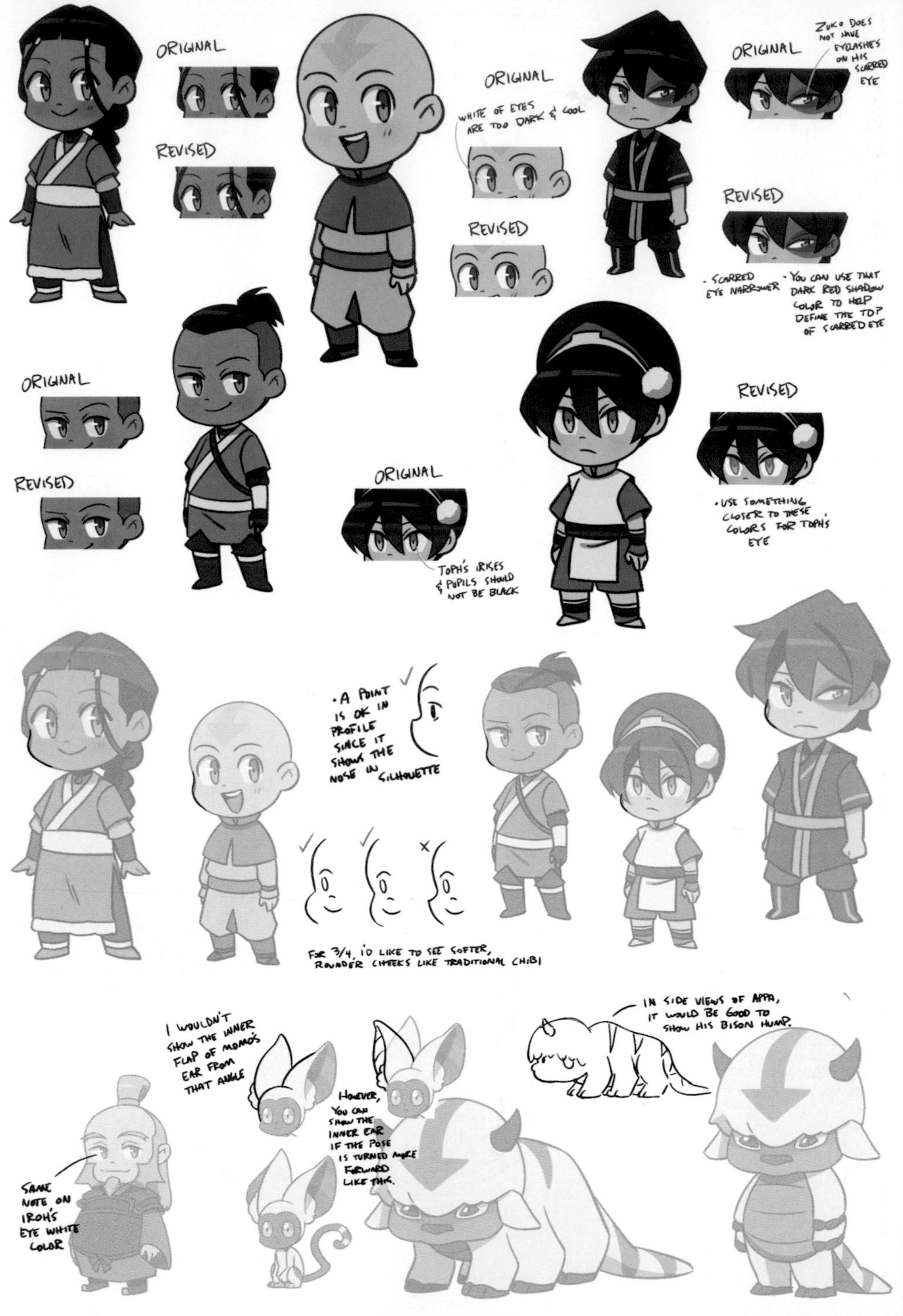
ORIGINAL
REVISED
ORIGINAL
WHITE OF EYES ARE TOO DARK & COOL
REVISED
ORIGINAL
ZUKO DOES NOT HAVE EYELASHES ON HIS SCARRED EYE
REVISED
- SCARRED EYE NARROWER
- YOU CAN USE THAT DARK RED SHADOW COLOR TO HELP DEFINE THE TOP OF SCARRED EYE
ORIGINAL
REVISED
ORIGINAL
TOPH'S IRISES & PUPILS SHOULD NOT BE BLACK
REVISED
• USE SOMETHING CLOSER TO THESE COLORS FOR TOPH'S EYE
• A POINT IS OK IN PROFILE SINCE IT SHOWS THE NOSE IN SILHOUETTE
FOR 3/4, I'D LIKE TO SEE SOFTER, ROUNDER CHEEKS LIKE TRADITIONAL CHIBI
I WOULDN'T SHOW THE INNER FLAP OF MOMO'S EAR FROM THAT ANGLE
HOWEVER, YOU CAN SHOW THE INNER EAR IF THE POSE IS TURNED MORE FORWARD LIKE THIS.
IN SIDE VIEWS OF APPA, IT WOULD BE GOOD TO SHOW HIS BISON HUMP.
SAME NOTE ON IROH'S EYE WHITE COLOR

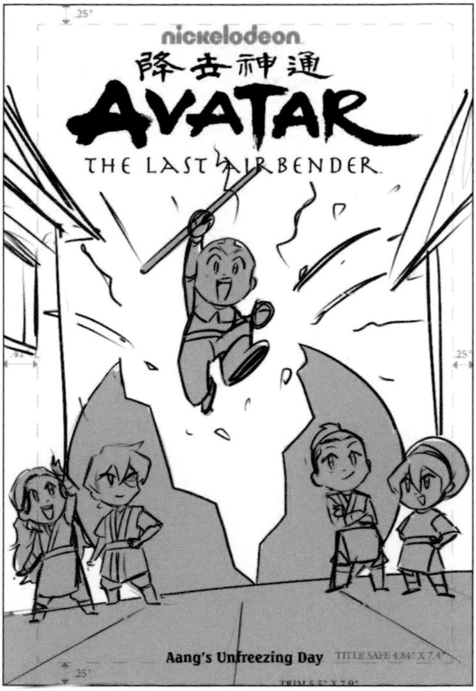
nickelodeon
AVATAR
THE LAST AIRBENDER
Aang's Unfreezing Day
TITLE SAFE 4.84" X 7.4"

Creating the cover takes many steps. First a sketch is made with the characters and action that will be featured . . .

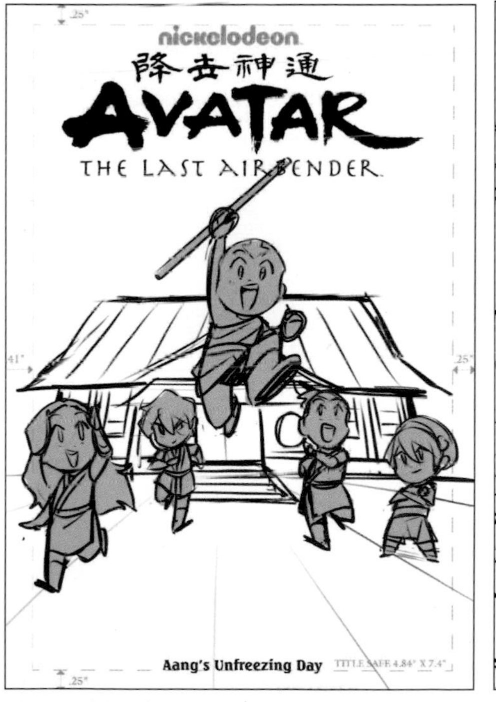
nickelodeon
AVATAR
THE LAST AIRBENDER
Aang's Unfreezing Day
TITLE SAFE 4.84" X 7.4"

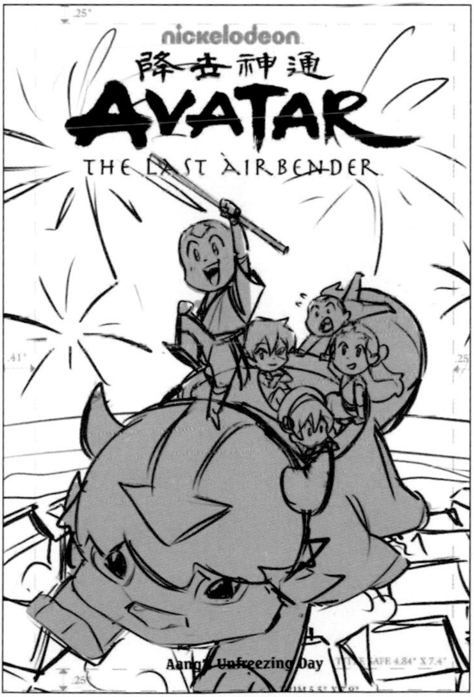
nickelodeon
AVATAR
THE LAST AIRBENDER

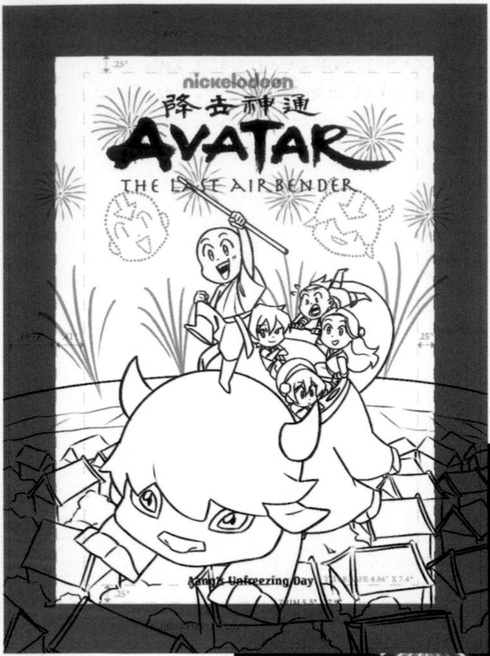
nickelodeon
AVATAR
THE LAST AIRBENDER
Aang's Unfreezing Day

. . . then the artist turns that into clean, smooth line art. After the line art is finished, color is added to really bring the cover to life!

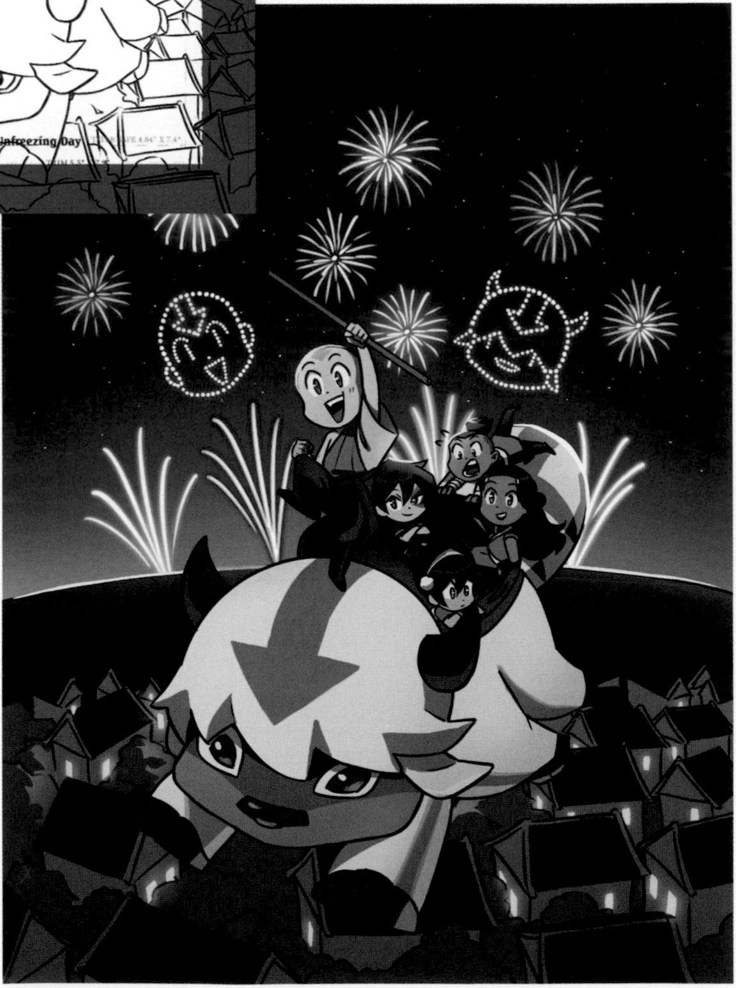

**Writing the script is the foundation for the whole comic! The writer decides how many panels (the boxes that make up comics) will be on each page and what will happen in each of them, as well as what characters will say. They have to decide what parts of the story will be communicated by words, and what will be communicated by the art.**

PAGE 5

PANEL 1
A large panel shows Toph doing another earthbending stance with the cart behind her. Aang is trying to walk around the side of the cart. He now is starting to look annoyed as a slab of earth pops up on the back of the cart, blocking his view again. Now three sides of the cart are blocked with earth slabs.

                    TOPH
     Just head back to the house like Sokka said.
            We'll come and get you later.

PANEL 2
Aang walks around the remaining side as another slab pops up on the remaining side. Aang is frustrated and confused.

                    AANG
            Come get me for what?

PANEL 3
Close up on Toph pausing looking nervous as she realizes she said too much.

PANEL 4
Toph earthbends. Behind her is the cart that has slabs of earth surrounding it. The earth under Aang bends up like a ribbon, raising him up in the air. He's surprised by this. It pushes him back away from the cart a bit.

                    TOPH
            Like I said, it's none of
          your business, Twinkle Toes!

                    AANG
                    WOAH!

**Using the script, the artist begins to sketch out each page and carefully draws the scene described in each panel. The right characters? Check. Backgrounds? Double check. Silly expressions? Triple check!**

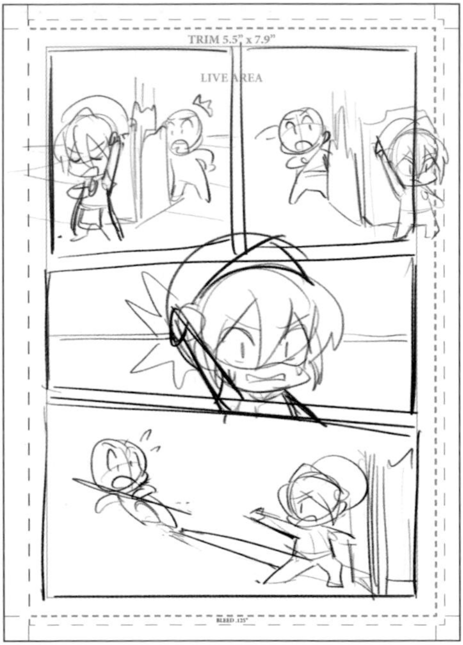
TRIM 5.5" x 7.9"
LIVE AREA
BLEED .125"

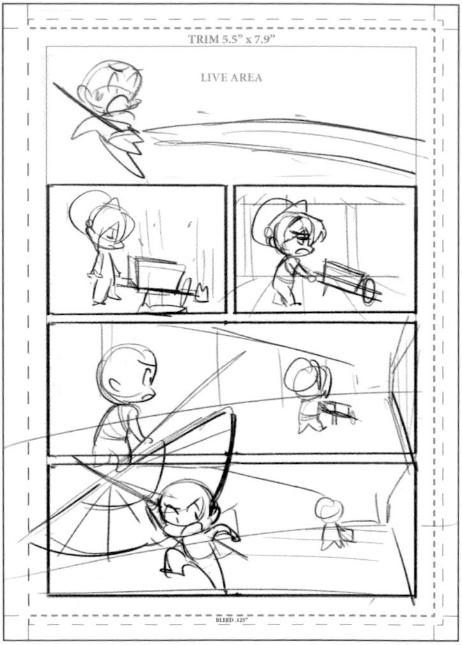
TRIM 5.5" x 7.9"
LIVE AREA
BLEED .125"

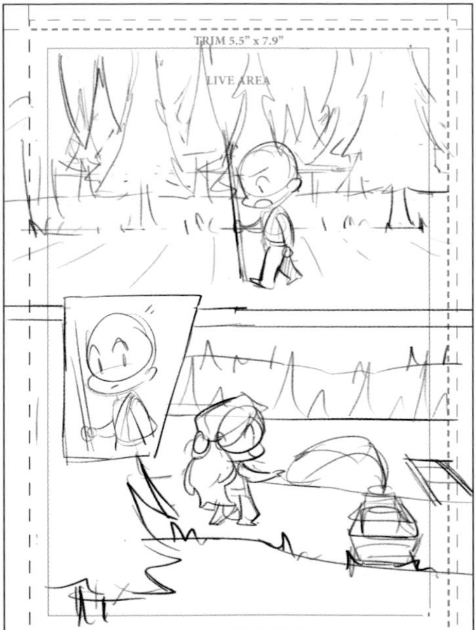
TRIM 5.5" x 7.9"
LIVE AREA
BLEED .125"

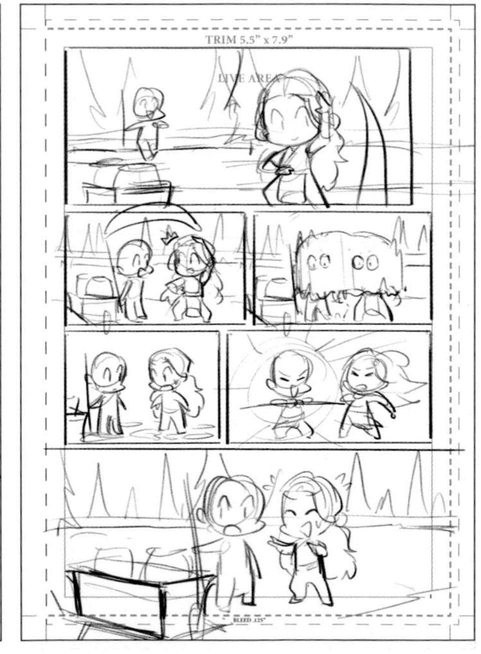
TRIM 5.5" x 7.9"
LIVE AREA
BLEED .125"

**Using the completed page sketches, or "thumbnails," as a guide, the artist begins to ink the drawings. Some artists ink with a pen and paper, but many artists ink digitally on a tablet.**

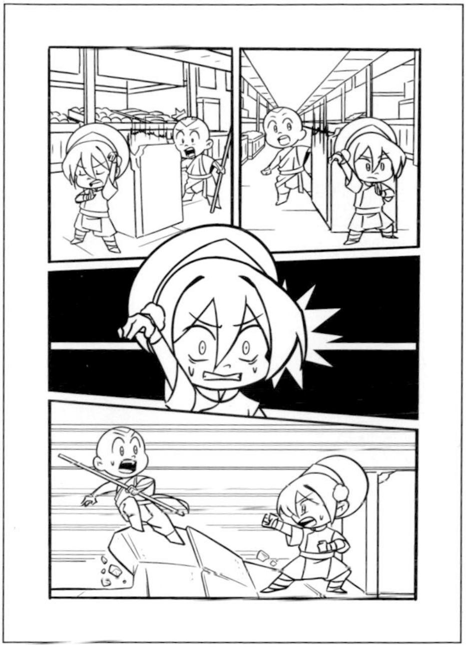

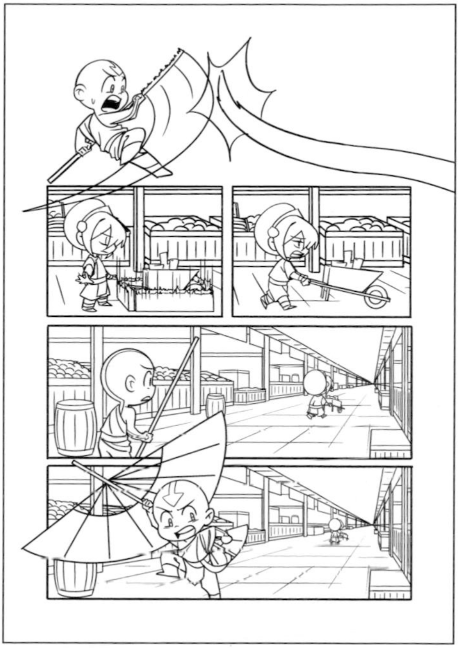

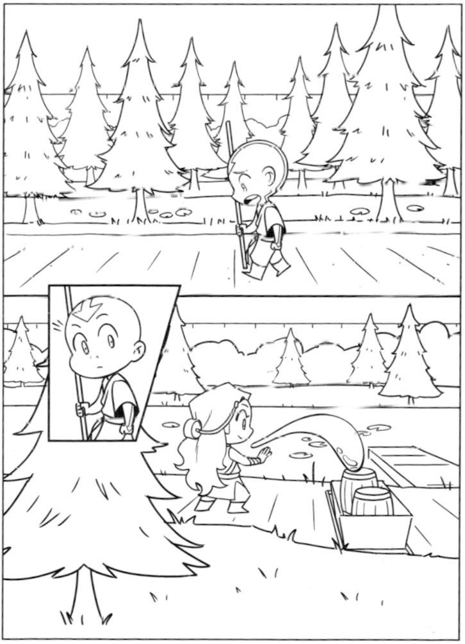

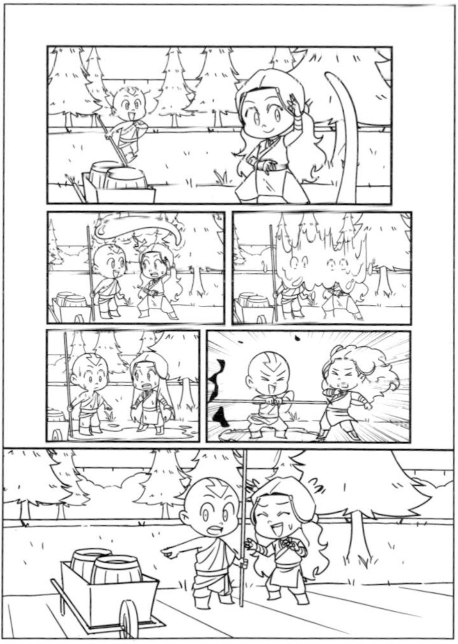

**After the art is inked, it's time to add colors! A colorist has to consider a lot of things like the time of day in the story, shapes and angles, and matching characters' palettes (or color guides) to their appearances elsewhere—like in the animated tv series!**

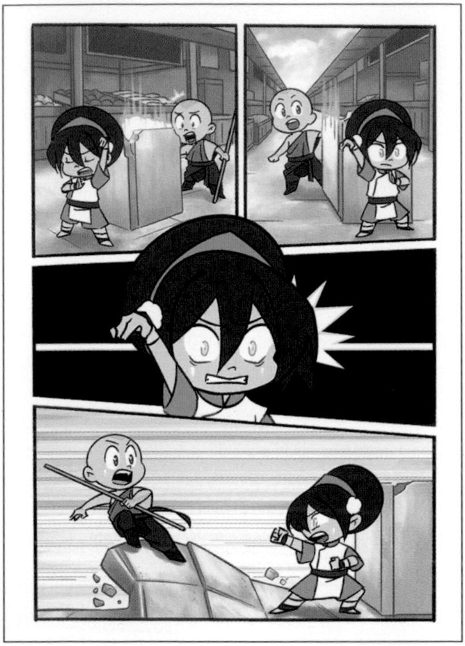

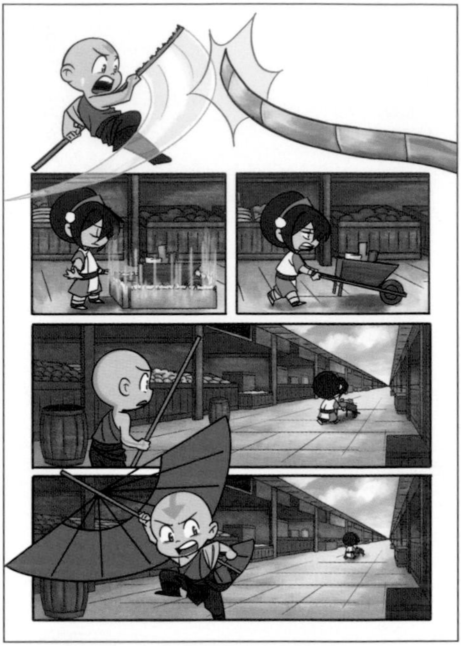

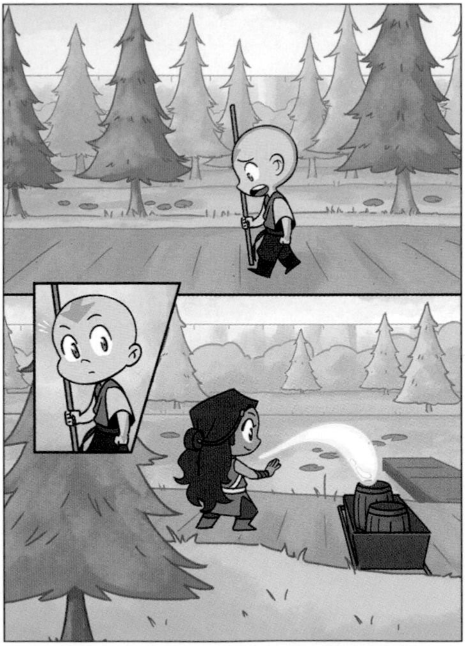

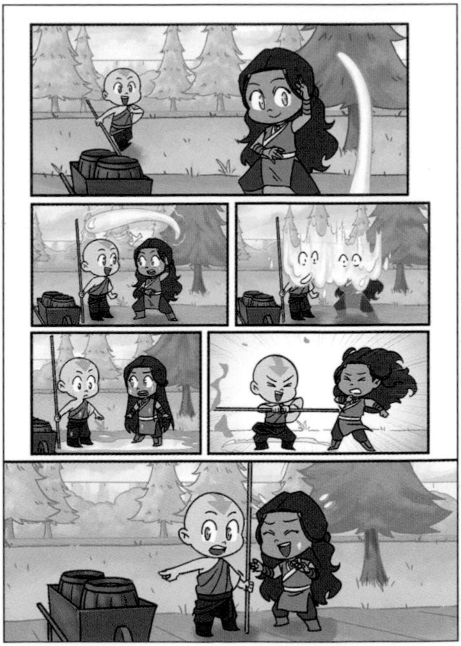

**Always leave room for lettering! This final step in the process combines the words and images of the comic to form a complete story!**

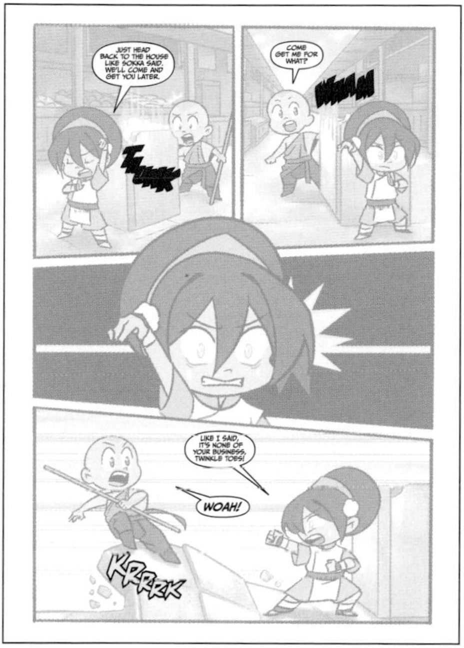
JUST HEAD BACK TO THE HOUSE LIKE SOKKA SAID. WE'LL COME AND GET YOU LATER.
THUNK
COME GET ME FOR WHAT?
LIKE I SAID, IT'S NONE OF YOUR BUSINESS, TWINKLE TOES!
WOAH!
KRRRK

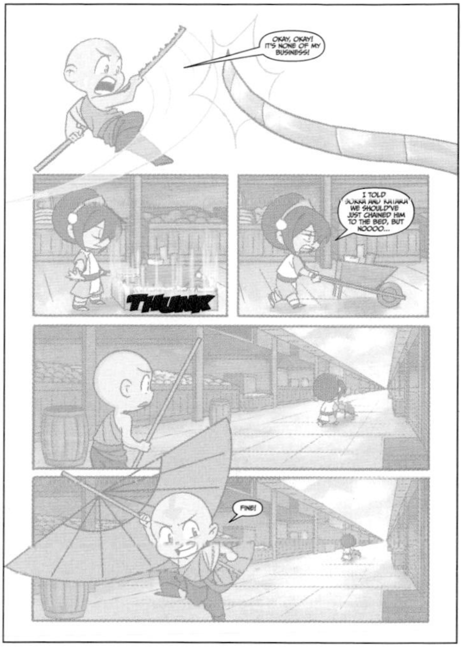
OKAY, OKAY! IT'S NONE OF MY BUSINESS!
THUNK
I TOLD SOKKA AND KATARA WE SHOULD'VE JUST CHAINED HIM TO THE BED, BUT NOOOO...
FINE!

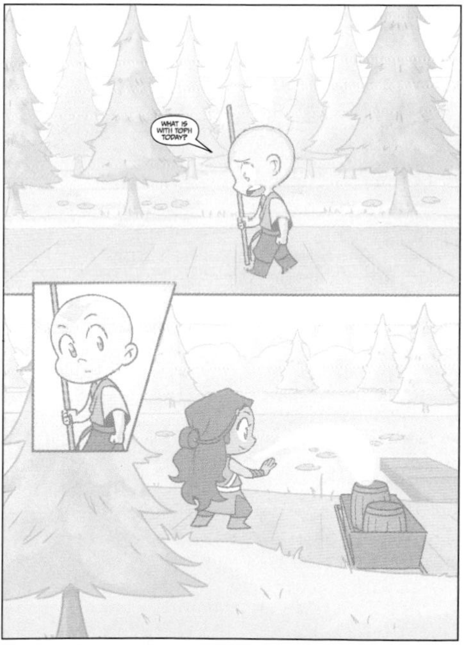
WHAT IS WITH TOPH TODAY?

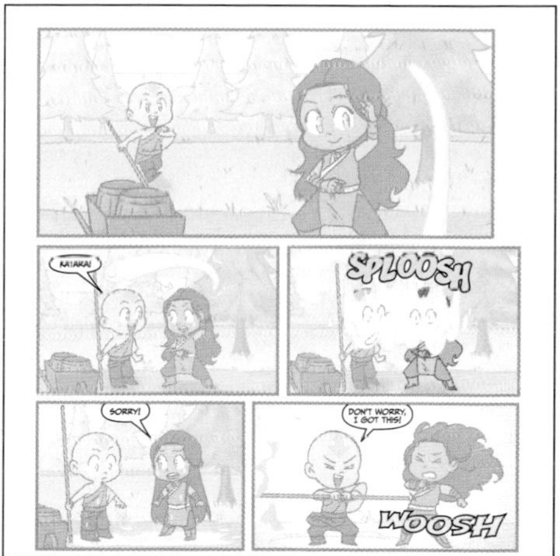
KATARA!
SPLOOSH
SORRY!
DON'T WORRY, I GOT THIS!
WOOSH
NEED SOME HELP WATERBENDING? WHAT ARE YOU DOING WITH THOSE BARRELS?
NOTHING! IT'S A WATER TRIBE THING. DON'T WORRY ABOUT IT. WHY ARE YOU IN TOWN?

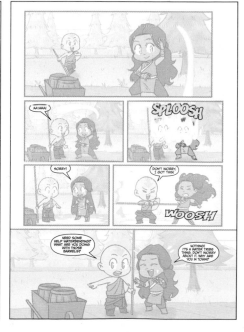

### And then, the best part: Read!
Making comics is a team effort, and so is enjoying them!
Share your favorite comics with a friend or loved one.
You could even work together to make your own!

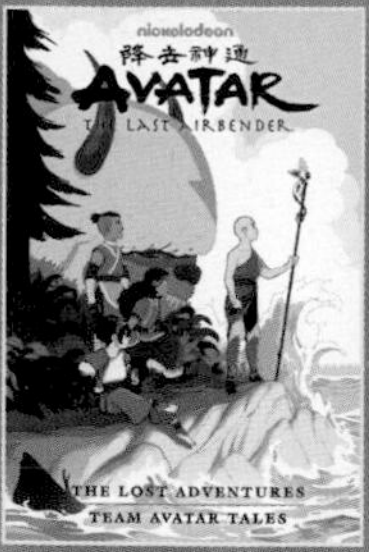
nickelodeon
AVATAR
THE LAST AIRBENDER
THE LOST ADVENTURES
TEAM AVATAR TALES

**Avatar: The Last Airbender—The Lost Adventures and Team Avatar Tales Library Edition**
978-1-50672-274-0 $39.99

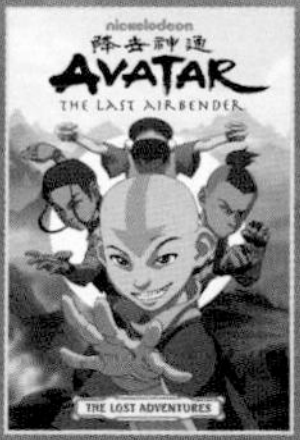
nickelodeon
AVATAR
THE LAST AIRBENDER
THE LOST ADVENTURES

**Avatar: The Last Airbender—The Lost Adventures**
978-1-59582-748-7 $19.99

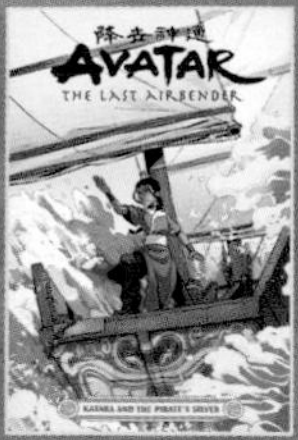
AVATAR
THE LAST AIRBENDER

**Avatar: The Last Airbender—Katara and the Pirate's Silver**
978-1-50671-711-1 $12.99

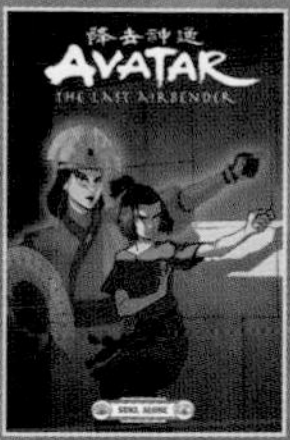
AVATAR
THE LAST AIRBENDER

**Avatar: The Last Airbender—Suki, Alone**
978-1-50671-713-5 $12.99

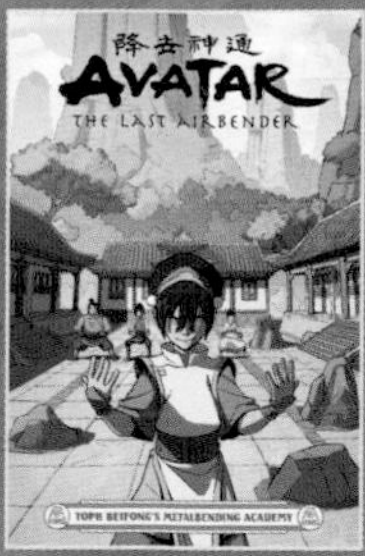
AVATAR
THE LAST AIRBENDER

**Avatar: The Last Airbender—Toph Beifong's Metalbending Academy**
978-1-50671-712-8 $12.99

nickelodeon

降去神通

# AVATAR

## THE LAST AIRBENDER™

## BE PART OF THE INCREDIBLE JOURNEY!

**Check out the best-selling graphic novels and recapture the magic!**

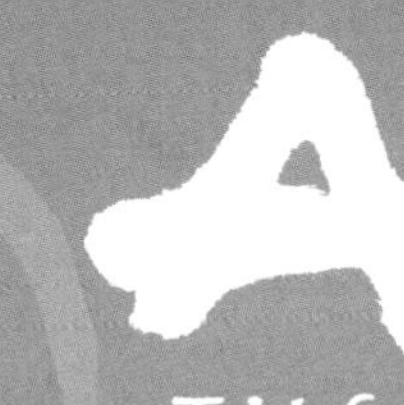
nickelodeon
降去神通
AVATAR
THE LAST AIRBENDER
THE ART OF THE ANIMATED SERIES

**Avatar: The Last Airbender—The Art of the Animated Series**
978-1-59582-504-9 $39.99

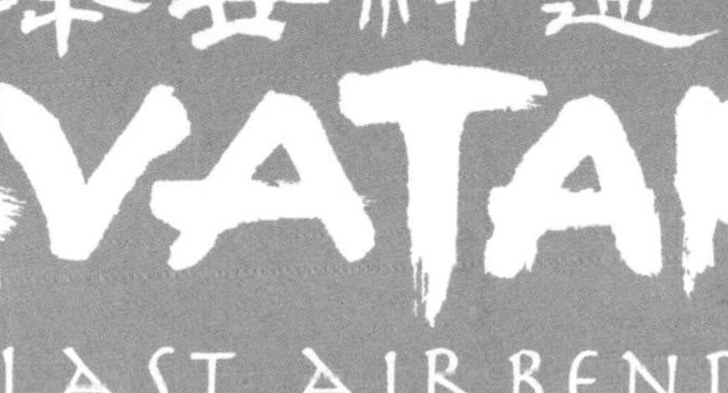
AVATAR
THE LAST AIRBENDER

**Avatar: The Last Airbender—Imbalance Part 1**
978-1-50670-489-0 $12.99

**Avatar: The Last Airbender—Imbalance Part 2**
978-1-50670-652-8 $12.99

**Avatar: The Last Airbender—Imbalance Part 3**
978-1-50670-813-3 $12.99

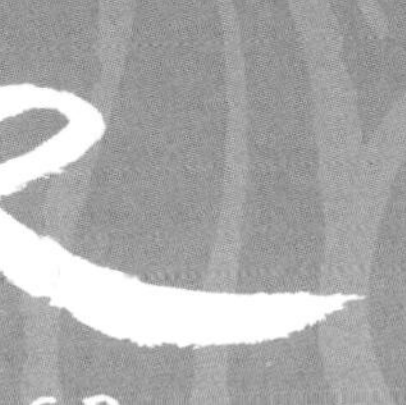
nickelodeon
AVATAR
THE LAST AIRBENDER
IMBALANCE

**Avatar: The Last Airbender—Imbalance Library Edition**
978-1-50670-812-6 $39.99

AVAILABLE AT YOUR LOCAL COMICS SHOP OR BOOKSTORE! To find a comics shop in your area, visit comicshoplocator.com. For more information or to order direct, visit DarkHorse.com

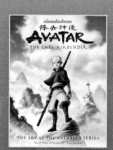

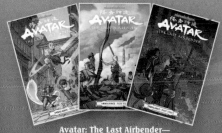

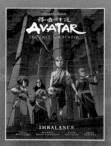

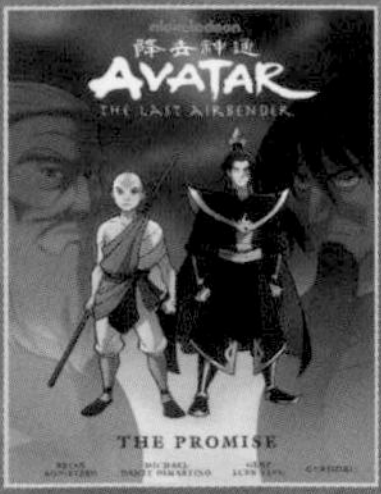
AVATAR
THE LAST AIRBENDER
THE PROMISE

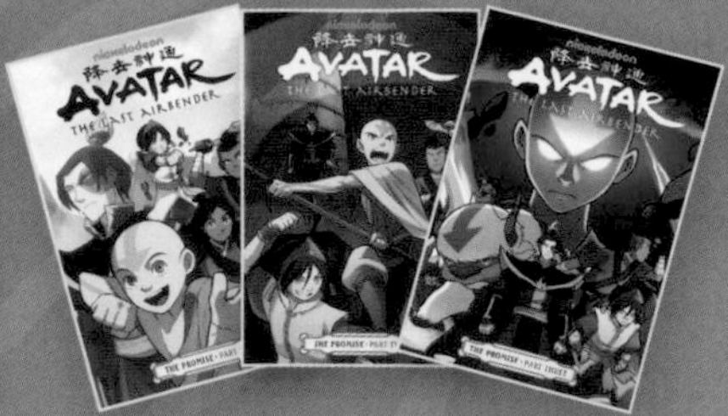

Avatar: The Last Airbender—
The Promise
Library Edition
978-1-61655-074-5 $39.99

Avatar: The Last Airbender—
The Promise Part 1
978-1-59582-811-8 $12.99

Avatar: The Last Airbender—
The Promise Part 2
978-1-59582-875-0 $12.99

Avatar: The Last Airbender—
The Promise Part 3
978-1-59582-941-2 $12.99

Avatar: The Last Airbender—
The Search
Library Edition
978-1-61655-226-8 $39.99

Avatar: The Last Airbender—
The Search Part 1
978-1-61655-054-7 $12.99

Avatar: The Last Airbender—
The Search Part 2
978-1-61655-190-2 $12.99

Avatar: The Last Airbender—
The Search Part 3
978-1-61655-184-1 $12.99

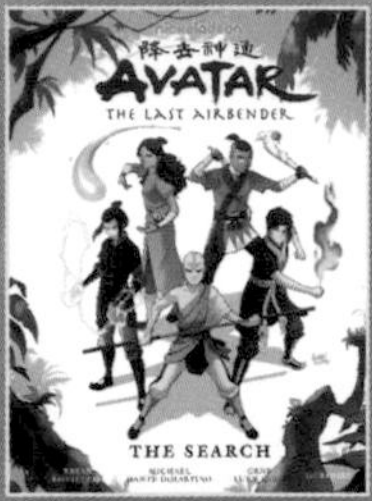
AVATAR
THE LAST AIRBENDER
THE SEARCH

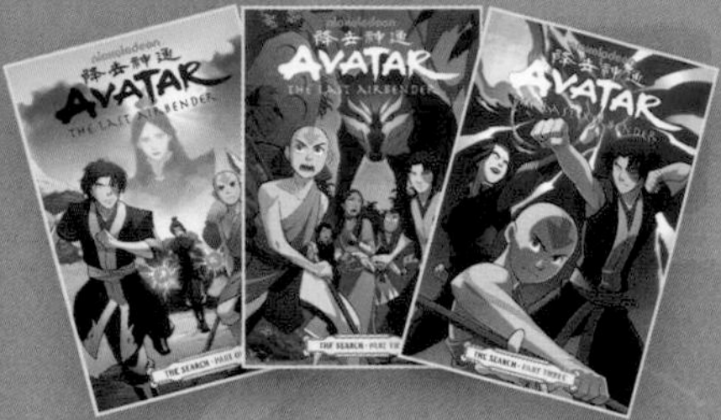

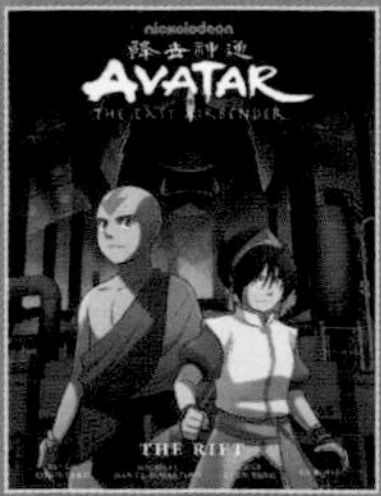
AVATAR
THE RIFT

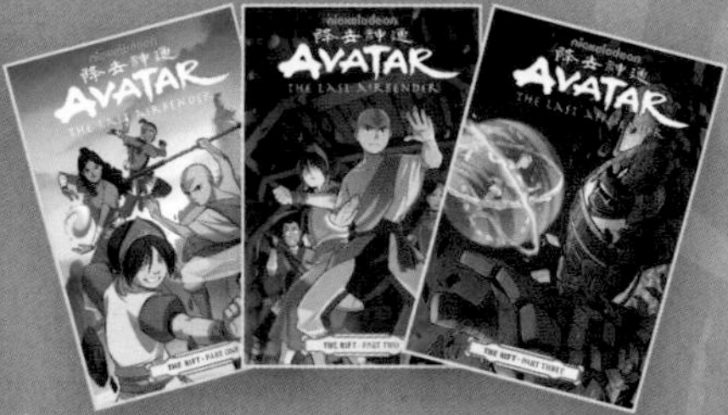

Avatar: The Last Airbender—
The Rift
Library Edition
978-1-61655-550-4 $39.99

Avatar: The Last Airbender—
The Rift Part 1
978-1-61655-295-4 $12.99

Avatar: The Last Airbender—
The Rift Part 2
978-1-61655-296-1 $12.99

Avatar: The Last Airbender—
The Rift Part 3
978-1-61655-297-8 $12.99

Avatar: The Last Airbender—
Smoke and Shadow
Library Edition
978-1-50670-013-7 $39.99

Avatar: The Last Airbender—
Smoke and Shadow Part 1
978-1-61655-761-4 $12.99

Avatar: The Last Airbender—
Smoke and Shadow Part 2
978-1-61655-790-4 $12.99

Avatar: The Last Airbender—
Smoke and Shadow Part 3
978-1-61655-838-3 $12.99

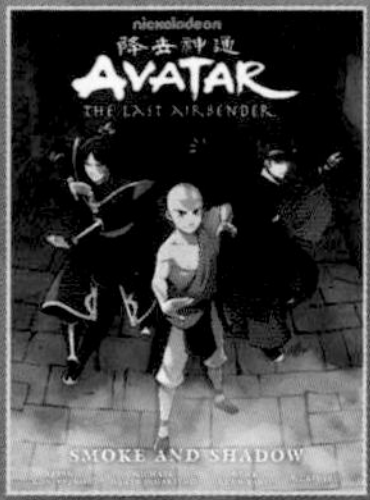
AVATAR
THE LAST AIRBENDER
SMOKE AND SHADOW

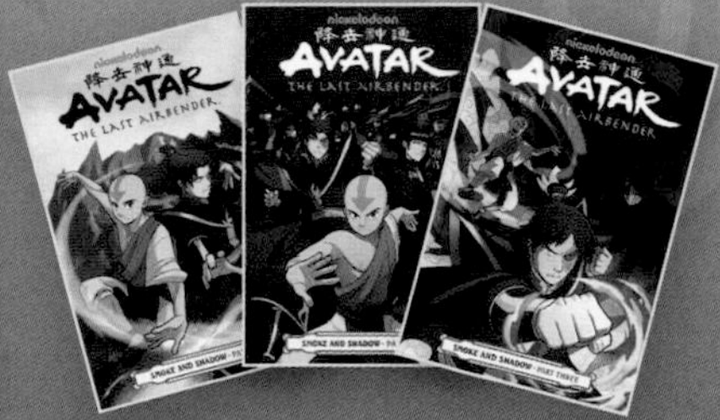

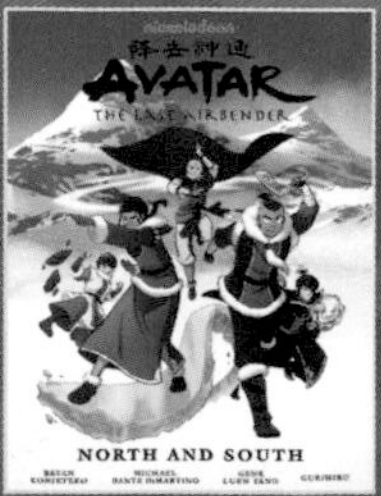
AVATAR
THE LAST AIRBENDER
NORTH AND SOUTH

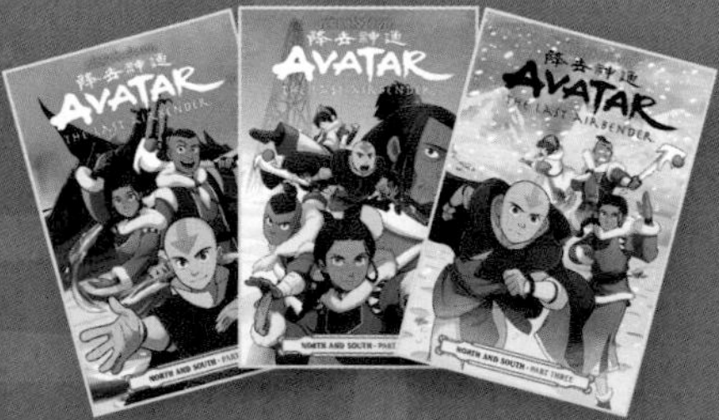

Avatar: The Last Airbender—
North and South
Library Edition
978-1-50670-195-0 $39.99

Avatar: The Last Airbender—
North and South Part 1
978-1-50670-022-9 $12.99

Avatar: The Last Airbender—
North and South Part 2
978-1-50670-129-5 $12.99

Avatar: The Last Airbender—
North and South Part 3
978-1-50670-130-1 $12.99